THE UNDESERVING BOSS

HASINA SAIYEDA

Think Tank™
Books

First published in 2020 by Think Tank Books™, New Delhi
Website: thinktankbooks.com
Email: editorial@thinktankbooks.com

Hasina Saiyeda asserts the moral right to be identified as the author of this book.

Copyright © Think Tank Books™
Copyright Text © 2020 by Hasina Saiyeda
Cover art by Tiyasa Mukherjee

This is a work of fiction. Names, characters, places and incidents are either the product of the author's imagination or are used fictitiously, and any resemblance to any actual persons, living or dead, events or locales, is entirely coincidental.

ISBN: 978-81-943705-2-9
Price: INR 225/-
Maximum retail price of this book listed is only for the Indian subcontinent. Selling price may vary elsewhere.

10 9 8 7 6 5 4 3 2 1

I seek the blessings of my grandparents.
I dedicate this book to my father, Syed MD Hafiz.

~~~About the Author~~~

Hasina Saiyeda is a Kolkata-based content writer who has a knack of telling stories to the world. She loves writing and contributes to blogs and other online platforms.

Being passionate about writing, she took it up as a profession and targets to share her ideas with larger audience. She writes in simple English so that everyone can read her stories. Her debut novel is 'Passion VS Parents… the game is on'. 'The Undeserving Boss' is her second novel.

~~~Acknowledgements~~~

First of all, thanks to my readers, for encouraging me to write my second novel.

Thanks a lot, to Think Tank Books and Gaurav Sharma for giving me a chance once more to prove myself. It's indeed more fun this time.

I would like to thank Tiyasa for designing the cover of the book with much attention. Tiyasa, you are such a lovely friend and a genius!

Thanks to mom for the awesome tea she makes that keeps me awake! Jokes apart, her support towards my writing career cannot be expressed in words.

Thanks to my father for giving an amazing life full of adventure, for trusting my choices, for supporting me in whatever I did in my 25 years of life. I'll make you prouder someday.

And, I have to thank my little brother, Haris and sister, Faria for all the love, care and respect they shower upon me. They are more enthusiastic than me whenever a new book comes out.

Thanks to Sahanaj, Saida, Sharifa, Suhana, and Hasib for keeping me motivated and positive while writing.

Thanks to Nabanita and Sunny for their constant support. They are the best friends one can have. And Sunny, you are always special!

I would like to thank the existing members of the Modern Computer Services for inspiring me to write this book. Here, I have more to learn…

Dear Diary,

Do you believe in God? I do. Well, it doesn't matter. What matters the most is how God treats you. Oh, no-no... I'm not complaining. I never complain. At least not before things went wrong- terribly wrong- with me. I was not forced into it. I chose it - the first choice I made for myself.

I could have gone out in my pyjamas, or lost all the online games with my friends, made disaster in my chemistry practical exam, broken my Mom's favourite home décor, slammed my Dad's bike to the iron gate we have, betrayed a friend, I could have gone for partying all night and come home drunk, or I could have sex with a random person in a random couch in a random house in a random party, I could have tripped over on my parents while they were having sex, I could have discovered my best friend's used condoms, I could have done a lot of things to embarrass myself. But no. I didn't do any of these. Instead, I joined my Dad's company, leaving a well-paying job and dreams of studying in a foreign university.

It is another day of my embarrassment.

Yours,
Ella

i

'You think you can handle this?' Kailash smirked at me. He was hovering over my shoulder, standing behind my back. He broke my concentration in regretting my decision in my personal diary. I closed the diary and tilted my face to look at him closely. Gosh... that was gutsy.

'Will you try to behave?' I said, trying hard to control my temper. He stood straight. He put his hands in his pocket and smirked again. Now at what... only he knows. I turned my chair to face him.

'See Kailash, if you think I can't handle this office just because I am a woman, you are wrong. I am amazed at your audacity.'

'I like to talk straight forward.' He said. 'This is an ocean, and you are not even fully a woman. You are still a girl. You are twenty-two? Maybe twenty-three?' he said in a calculative way.

'Twenty-four.' I said. He was disgusting.

'You look like eighteen. Nobody is going to take you seriously here. Trust me.'

'They must take me seriously.' I turned away. Even I wasn't sure about what I was saying. 'And talking about that, Kailash, you are the only one who has a problem with me.'

'Others are not true to you.'

'Oh.' I gasped. 'Who else has a problem with me? Ali, Sudhir, or Nehal? Or Amar?'

'Maybe your close ones?'

I turned back to look at him again. He was standing just like before. Tall. Straight. Muscular. And obviously, rude and arrogant.

'Are you talking about Aarav?' I was shocked. I was not ready to believe that. He just smirked again.

'You know what, Kailash...' I got up from my chair. 'You can't handle the fact that your new boss is a twenty-four years old "girl".' I leaned towards him. 'Let me be clear to you Kailash. When I decided to sit in this chair, I did it after thinking a hundred times. I had promised this chair that I will always respect it. MUSE has 20 years of reputation in the market, and it will continue to be like that forever. Maybe some staff will get out of it, someday.'

'Are you threatening me? You can't fire anyone, you know, right?' he smirked again. I thought of hitting his eyes with the tweezers.

'Good Night, Kailash. Go home.' I pulled my bag and left the office with big steps.

I was just trying to learn. I was on an unofficial 'training mode' in MUSE set up by my father, the founder, owner, and CEO of MUSE. He wants to hand the company over to me after a few years if I prove myself worthy of the job. Yes, then I can fire anyone I want. I can fire this irritating Kailash as well. But I didn't join MUSE to fire anyone.

I crossed the lane that has great glory in traffic jams. This road leads to Chowringhee, now called Jawaharlal Nehru Road, a glorious location in Kolkata. I watched a Bengali movie of the same name a few days back and I liked it. How beautiful life would have been if it was a movie? I am not a Bengali. However, I can talk in Bengali and read Bengali. I can write it as well. I have been interested in learning new languages since childhood. It is another thing that my Dad got my interest in. French is the new language I was learning those days.

Kolkata is a growing city, and the lanes are getting busier as it is developing every day. I saw office-returnees. I saw busy men and women trying to cross each other on the road. Everybody wants to reach home as soon as possible. Everyone is in a hurry. But my feet stopped. Kailash's smirk bothered me a lot. For seven days, he did not speak a single word to me except for work. And today, he spoke it up all at once. Though I knew that he didn't like my presence in Dad's place much.

Why did I decide to take this on my shoulder? I had time. I am just twenty-four. I had a dream of doing an MBA abroad after the job.

I felt stupid standing at the busiest road of Kolkata. My feet started moving slowly. You can't just stand idle here - everyone moves fast. You should keep moving, no matter what. Because if you don't move, you will be left alone in the middle of the odds and unknowns.

I pulled up in a small outlet, asked for a cigarette and lit it like a pro. I am not a regular smoker. But I become a pro when I get tensed or excited. I paid for the cigarette and headed towards the main road.

By the way, I am Ella. Well, it's not my actual name. But my close ones call me by this name. Even I like it. I am the eldest daughter of my father. He single-handedly founded Modernus Enterprise, famous as MUSE, twenty years ago. A service provider company in the software and hardware sector; mainly hardware. A company that has retained its glory since it was established. A company that deals with its customers most impressively and professionally. A company that has a brighter future. A company that is fierce competition for others of the same kind.

It was all okay, and normal until my grandmother called me one day and said, 'Your father had two biggest dreams in his life. You know what they are?' I had mentioned a clear 'no', to which she replied, 'To establish his own company, and to see it run the same way forever.' That was the first time when I realized what MUSE meant to Dad. There were some inside stories too that I discovered with time.

I am not my parents' only daughter, as I said. They have one more, Kaira - my sister, who is three years younger than me and currently pursuing her M.Sc. in Mathematics. Kaira always wanted to become a mathematics scholar. She was always passionate about it, and she proved that her passion is justified. On the other hand, I am passionate about technology. Shoot! That was enough for my Dad to identify his successor.

After I finished my Engineering from a reputed college and managed to get a decent job as a software developer, a rumor spread in my family like fire. I started hearing the same thing now and then. It was "Only Ella can handle MUSE after her Dad." Well, everyone did not think so. My cousin, Shadab always felt that he would be the next successor of MUSE as he is the only son in our generation.

My extended family was determined to make me leave everything and dedicate my life to MUSE. On the other hand, they were forcing Shadab to become a little sensitive so that he could help me in MUSE. For the people in my family, it was quite clear. If Shadab fails, I'll handle MUSE and train him until I get married and leave everything to him. If I fail, Shadab had a clear way to become the next CEO of MUSE. Shadab is two years younger to me and does nothing productive in his life, ever!

Things took a twist when my Dad got sick for a week and admitted to the hospital. At 55, his health started showing its true color sometimes. He needed a backup now for MUSE. He needed to lower his work stress, and for that, a successor was needed immediately. Shadab was initially put into work. In a week, he started throwing tantrums and went back to his shell. Well, that was a year ago.

I was at the top of my career when all this happened. I finished cigarettes one after another but couldn't convince myself to leave a software development job just to sit in my Dad's chair at this young age. I was scared. I considered myself too young and inexperienced for this.

All eyes were on me, and my eyes were blank. I wanted to go abroad to study MBA. I was twenty-three then, and Dad had never forced me to join MUSE, leaving everything behind. He knew that MUSE was the last place I would want myself to be. But I knew that if anyone could handle MUSE after Dad, it was only me, Ella.

ii

'Ella, get up. It's 8 O' Clock, girl.' Mom shook me tremendously. I opened my eyes but couldn't figure anything out. Where was I?

'Ella, you are getting late for office, dear.'

OFFICE! Say like this, no? It's not an office. It's an ocean where I was just a tiny creature. Or maybe just a girl, not even a woman whom nobody takes seriously.

I never got up at 8 AM since I left school. I always get up after ten. Even my office used to start at eleven, and I used to rush every day. It's obvious, I never arrived on time. But this is MUSE. It opens at 10 AM and starts operating from 10:15. MUSE is always punctual, no matter what.

'Everything all right there?' Dad asked me at the breakfast table.

'Yes.' I said quickly. I didn't say anything about Kailash's threat because I wanted to handle him myself.

'Try to know your clients properly, even if they are annoying.' He said. 'A good businessman always knows his clients well.'

'I am trying, Dad.' I said, biting the bread sandwich lightly.

'Plus, your staff, godown members, and suppliers are also important. Try to interact with them as much as you can.' Dad said. I nodded.

'Are you enjoying it?' Mom asked. This question made me think a bit.

'Absolutely,' I smiled answering to Mom after few seconds. 'It was absolutely my decision to leave the MBA prep and dedicate myself to MUSE. I am completely ready to handle everything no matter what comes in my way.'

'I'm proud of you, Ella.' Mom smiled with tears of joy in her eyes. 'It's going to be your company sooner or later. You have to take care of everything.'

'It will always be Dad's company or whoever he chooses later. I am just the baton bearer for now.' I said. Dad smiled, sipping his tea. Mom brushed her hand over my head.

'Okay, I have to get ready.' I said. 'I should be punctual.'

'Yes. You should always maintain MUSE's policy. And discipline is the most important one.' Dad reminded me again for the nth time.

I sipped my tea softly. Tea and I have a perfect relationship that starts with the heart and ends up on the lips. Even I don't share this kind of relationship with Haris, my best friend. He is the closest person I have. We share everything, and everybody has to doubt that we may end up marrying each other. Well, we didn't think about that though. Or maybe he did. But I didn't. Well, that's not the story, c'mon.

'Ella,' Dad's voice made me realize that my tea was getting cold, I sipped it again with so much of love.

'Yes, Dad?'

'Remember that MUSE is an ocean.' I spit the remaining tea in my mouth.

'What happened?' Mom and Dad said together. 'Are you okay?' Mom added, getting up to help me.

'I'm absolutely fine.' I said. 'Yes, Dad.' I turned to my father, who was staring at my face. 'I'll always remember that.' I flashed a smile at him and left for my room.

This was my eighth day in MUSE and I was already spitting out food. I was already facing a lot of challenges that I didn't want my father to trace. But he would somehow come to know someday for sure. If he doesn't, I am a genius.

Joining MUSE was a sudden decision. It was as accidental as Dr. Manmohan Singh becoming the Prime Minister of India.

It was a busy day. I had left the job in December because I wanted to prepare for a foreign university to do an MBA. I was searching for home-based work and almost cracked one. So, I had no financial shortage as well.

Sometime in February, I was having dinner with my parents as usual. We always have dinner together.

There, a small conversation took place that made me land in MUSE.

'We have 30% less success rate from the last month on Monitors and MotherBoards repairing. Our company depends on repairing our customer's product and make them trust us in this. Even laptops have 20% less success rate than the previous month.' Dad mumbled between mutton pieces.

'Why?' Mom asked him, worried.

'There's one probable reason but I am not sure of it.' Dad said.

'What's that?'

'Irregularity.' Dad said. 'The engineers are not delivering their work on time. We are losing customers. Plus the suppliers are not supplying materials that are required to repair the hardware components.' He paused. Mom and I stared at his face. 'We lost two RAMs last month as well. Neither Ali knows about them nor Aarav. And Kailash doesn't even care about anything. Two RAMs do not cost much, but the humiliation I faced cannot be explained in words!' He added, shaking his head.

'Why didn't you enquire deeply about it? It's a loss in business.' Mom said to Dad. She stopped eating.

'Yes, clear loss.' I commented.

'But what will I do?' Dad said. 'I don't have proof.'

'Dad, you don't need any proof to enquire them.'

'I don't think Ali would do it. He is the most trustworthy person in the office. He is very well-behaving, Ella.' Dad said proudly. His eyes glittered.

'What about Aarav and Kailash?'

'Aarav respects me a lot. Why would he steal? Kailash is irresponsible but not a threat to business.' Dad said. 'Talking about Nehal, Amar, and Sudhir... I don't know about their intentions.'

'Then where did the RAMs go, Dad?' I asked.

'I don't know.'

'Did it happen before?'

'Maybe. It's very tough to keep track of everything alone, you know. If Shadab would have been there...' he stopped.

'You have to be very regular to stop all these.' Mom said to Dad. 'If you don't go to office daily the business will go down. An outsider cannot be responsible for the theft. It's someone among them only.'

'That's not possible now. I am 56. I have an allergy to dust and it troubles me every day. I have diabetes. I am getting weaker day by day. I cannot take much pressure at this age.' Dad shook his head. 'There was a time when I didn't care about anything and anyone. I worked day and night to build this business. I did my best to make MUSE stand straight. But now...'

He left the sentence hanging. Nobody was speaking now. Nobody was eating either. Kaira stared at her food silently. Mom was tensed - it was visible on her face. Dad was in deep thought. I kept on scanning everyone's probable expression.

'What will happen then? MUSE is all we have. What if it loses its reputation and glory?' Mom broke the silence after almost a minute that seemed like a decade.

'I can't let that happen.' Dad said. 'I want someone to appoint at MUSE like my eyes. I want someone reliable. I can't trust Shadab. He can't even keep track of orders. I want a baton bearer now who can run MUSE as I did.'

The last sentence made me think. 'Baton bearer'. I repeated in my mind. I finished my food. I went to the sink to wash my hands.

'I don't know what will happen. It's not a good sign, whatever it is.' Mom said. 'Are we losing customers?'

Dad nodded. It indicated 'yes'. I watched everything from the sink area. The water flowed on. I kept on applying handwash in my hands. Deep inside, my mind was planning something now.

'A business without a customer is a dump yard.' Dad mumbled after a few seconds. The tap caught my attention now. I quickly washed my hands and turned it off.

'MUSE can't be a dump yard, Dad.' I prompted coming back to the dining table. I stood by its side between Mom and Dad. 'We can figure something out.' They all looked at me. They didn't take me seriously. I understood it and went inside my room bidding 'good night' to Mom and Dad and punching on Kaira's back. She didn't punch me back like she always does. She was quiet. I went to bed and dialed Haris.

'Hey, you didn't call me all evening. What's wrong?' he asked.

'I was busy with a code. I am working on a website, you know.' I said.

'Yes, I know. Did they pay you?'

'50%,' I said, 'rest after work. I have to deliver it tomorrow.'

'Don't stress out. It's okay, you can do it. You are a genius.' He smiled at the other side on the phone. I knew it.

'Haris, I think I am not just made for coding websites. I have something more to do. Something different. Something more respectful.'

'Do you want to open an NGO?' he chuckled.

'Let me save my boat first.' I mumbled.

'What happened, Ella? You sound serious.' He sensed it finally.

'MUSE needs me, I guess.'

'I told you that a year ago. You are your Dad's first child. You have some responsibility, dude.'

'Don't call me dude.' I complained like every time. He chuckled. I added, 'Yes. Everybody close to me said so at least once.'

'Ella, it's an empire that your Dad established. Now it is your turn to run it. Shadab already made a disaster a year ago. You can't depend on him anymore. He can help in future if he gets serious... but that's a different discussion.'

I kept quiet. Actually, I lacked vocabulary.

'But why did you suddenly think of it?' he asked.

'MUSE is going through a bad phase. Dad can't be regular there. His diabetes is not under control. Last month also, he was hospitalized for three days. I have to become his eye in MUSE. Plus he needs a baton bearer now.'

'Did he tell you anything?'

'No. But I know what he wants. He will never tell me to leave my job and dreams to get confined in MUSE. He knows that I left the job to do an MBA.'

'That's right. He cares for your dreams, unlike other parents. He never forces you to do anything.'

'Hmm... Haris... what should I do?'

'Join MUSE from tomorrow.'

I kept quiet. I knew he would say that only.

'My dream of going abroad for an MBA has to be dropped. Haris, life will completely change. I will be confined in four walls of MUSE forever.'

'Ella, Ella, Ella... listen to me. You may don't need MUSE, but MUSE needs you. After 10 years if you look back to this day, you would not have any regret. I guarantee you that.' He said. 'MUSE is a heritage for your family. You are lucky to be chosen as a successor.' He added. 'They could have picked Kaira or your cousin, Shadab, who is good for nothing. Or anybody. But your Dad only trusts you but nobody. You know what that means?'

'I think I'm getting to know.' I said.

'Each one of your family believes in you, Ella.' He added. 'At least, after Shadab failed last year. They may not want you there forever. But you have to join MUSE and prove that you are the most capable one. You may go through financial problems now. You won't get paid for joining MUSE as well. It's not a job anymore. It's total responsibility. MUSE is huge for you, I know. But trust me, MUSE has only one proper guide after your Dad. That's you.'

'Should I join from tomorrow?' I asked.

'Sure. What are you waiting for?'

'But I have to talk to Dad first. Plus Dad needs to announce it first in the office.'

'Tell your Dad about it the first thing in the morning.' He said. 'Let him handle the formalities.'

'Yeah.' I whispered.

'Ella,' he called affectionately. 'Don't worry.'

'I am a little scared.' I said. 'It's a men's world. Have you ever seen a woman in the hardware sector? Plus, there's not a single woman in my family who is given this kind of responsibility.'

'Shut up. There's nothing like this.' He laughed. 'You don't need an example. Do your work in your way.'

'Will they accept me as their boss?' I asked.

'Try to be their friend first. I know it's unprofessional. But you are too young to be a boss.'

'Hmm.'

'Okay, sleep now. Tomorrow is important for you. And please don't change your mind at the last moment. That's the one and the only bad habit of you.'

'I think I can trust me this time.'

'Finger crossed. Love you, Ella. I am proud of your decision today. Bye'

'Bye. Good Night, Haris.'

'I'm proud of you, *sherni*.' He chuckled. I smiled.

After that, it happened so fast…

I informed Dad about my joining. He couldn't believe me sometimes. He even said that I had a nightmare. Mom assured him that I could handle MUSE.

Mom supported me positively. And finally, I got dressed up the other day and went to the office.

iii

'Good Morning, Ma'am.' Aarav smiled at me. He is one inch taller than me. I am 5'4". It is more manageable for me to look at his eyes.

'Good Morning.' My eye rested on his deep eyes for a brief second. He was my father's secretary. Now, my secretary.

Aarav is one year younger than me. He is a computer science graduate who was badly looking for a job one year ago. His father, a military person, suddenly passed away few years ago. His mother suffers from chronic disease. She came to Kolkata from Delhi after her husband's death. Aarav is the only son. My Dad hired him so that he could support his family.

In the last seven days, I have cultivated Aarav a lot. In Dad's absence, I needed a guide who would teach me how MUSE works. Aarav was the perfect person in this case. Every time I made a mistake, he would smile briefly turning his fair cheeks red. That was adorable for sure.

'Okay, that would be Pentium IV, not Pentium III. You have low knowledge of hardware as you are a software student. But you are learning fast.' He smiled. I looked at him briefly. His cheeks turned red. His eyes sparkled. He avoided eye contact with me all the time. I didn't know why... okay... initially, I didn't.

Well, I was fond of Aarav already. Not because he was assisting me like an angel. Not because he had accepted me as his boss already, or he was trying to keep me motivated all the time. Not because he was teaching me the difference between DDR2 and DDR3 RAM or identification of Pentium III and Pentium IV. Not because he was meticulous for me from the first hour I joined MUSE. Not because he respects me so much. It's because he looks like a person whom I loved once and lost because of a lot of misunderstandings.

That's some spice... eh? That's undoubtedly a spicy twist in my story so far. But that's not a very good thing for me. I sometimes hated to look at him even. I have heard that seven people in the world look identical. Two of them of the same kind are in my life. Impressive!

'Do you think I can handle MUSE?' I asked Aarav. He was busy with some files, so he did not lift his face.

'I think you can learn everything by the rainy season. We do some real business in the rainy season.'

'Thanks for having faith in me.' I chuckled.

'You are very brave, Ma'am.' He said.

'Why do you think so?' I asked.

'If I were in your place, I would never dare take this responsibility. It's not taking over a ration shop.'

'Don't scare me.' I laughed.

'Am I scaring you?'

'Yes.' I said.

He laughed. 'Sorry, Ma'am. But that's the truth.'

'May I come in?' A voice came from the door. We both lifted our face to look at him. We knew the voice.

'Yes, Kailash. Come in.' I said.

'How's everything here... Ma'am?' he said, looking at me intensely.

'Fine.' I said. 'What's the matter?' I asked. He stood in front of me. 'I think we have some urgent jobs in your account.'

'I have a doubt.' He said. 'The LCD I am working on needs more materials. The expense will be more than the usual one.'

'We have to ask the customer, in that case, I guess.' I looked at Aarav.

'Yes.' Aarav responded.

'Cool. Get back to your desk. I am letting you know.' I said. He left.

'Aarav, I'll call. Not you. I have to know my customers.'

'Fine, Ma'am.' He said, instructing me to make the call. I did it. He complimented me for doing it well.

'Aarav, fix a meeting with the staff tomorrow at 11 AM.' I told him.

'Okay, Ma'am.' He said.

'And let Kailash know about the customer's decision. He agreed to go with it. Tell him to make a list of the extra materials. We need to report to the customer.' I said. I took the phone up to call Sudhir, the godown manager.

'Okay, Ma'am.' Aarav picked up the phone to call Kailash.

'Hello.' Sudhir's voice rang up in my ear. 'Good Morning, Ma'am.'

'Good morning, Sudhir.' I said. 'Kailash needs some extra materials. He will give you the list. Please help him.'

'Ma'am, the godown is not in good condition. We are not getting supplies.' He said on the phone.

'Why?'

'They are asking for bulk orders. And we don't order in bulk.'

'I'll talk to Dad regarding this.' I assured him and made a point in my notebook. I have a habit of forgetting small things. However, it's a significant matter for MUSE.

'Ma'am,' he paused, 'can I come to meet you in the office?'

'Sure.' I said. 'Come up.'

Sudhir has been handling the godown in MUSE for eight years. Dad didn't even look at the godown business. By now, I knew that among others, Dad trusted Sudhir as well. Basically, Dad believed everyone.

I leaned back on my chair. For 20 years, Dad sat on this chair. Now he comes mostly on Saturdays. When he comes, I shift to a different chair. The chair suits Dad's personality, not mine. Maybe I need another 20 years to make myself look good in that chair. But will I stay for twenty years?

'Ma'am, the meeting has been fixed with Ali, Kailash, and Nehal.' Aarav broke my train of thoughts.

'What about Amar?' I said.

'He's an intern, Ma'am...'

'I need him as well.' I said. 'He has come here to learn something. This meeting is a part of it. Call everyone except for Sudhir and godown employees.'

'Does Sir know about this meeting, Ma'am?'

'No.' I said. 'I'll let him know tonight.'

He nodded. 'I'm informing Amar.' I showed him a thumbs-up sign.

'May I come in, Ma'am?' A man in a blue turban and thick beard asked me from the door of my cabin. He was in his mid-thirties.

'Come in.' I said, smiling.

'How are you, Ma'am?' he said after folding his hands to greet me. I also folded my hands in response. 'I am fine. How are you, Sudhir?' He just nodded, smiling.

'Sit.' I pointed to the chair across me. He sat down. He was wearing a white shirt that fit his body perfectly. His black trousers had white patches in many places. Maybe dirt. Godown is not exactly a very clean spot. The godown is located in the basement of the main building of MUSE. When MUSE was just a small shop of 10 feet by 12 feet, there was no such place called godown. Ten years ago, MUSE shifted to this new spot. It is now a two-storey building with a basement. Initially, Dad handled the godown. He ultimately left it for Sudhir after he joined.

Sudhir put his hands on the table. He cleared his throat.

'Ma'am, the godown is not in good condition. For a month, the suppliers are very irregular in supplying.

Many of them want bulk orders. Plus, the godown staff is asking for increment. They talked with sir.'

'I know about this, Sudhir. But MUSE is not in a condition to make an increment for godown staff. We have engineers here, we have cleaner, watchman…'

'I understand, Ma'am,' he cut me off, 'sorry for interrupting you.'

'It's okay.' I prompted.

'The godown staff do not have any complaint against anyone, Ma'am. But they deserve increment. Whose family runs in just INR 8,000 per month, Ma'am?'

'I'll talk about it to Dad.' I said and quickly wrote it on my notebook again. He saw that and smiled.

'Sudhir, do you have any idea about the theft last month?' I asked. 'We lost some properties, and the customers humiliated Dad.'

'I know about it. I was not there but I heard about it later. It's unfortunate.' He said. 'I can guarantee you that my godown staff did not do it. They will never do such a thing.'

'You mean to say that someone from the office did it?'

'There's a possibility.' He said. 'But I don't know anyone here. I talk and report to Aarav whenever your father is absent.'

I kept quiet. He also sat quietly, looking at his hands on the table.

'Anything else you want to say?' I broke the silence.

'Ma'am, there's a lot of spare items in the godown. Please make an arrangement to sell them off. Plus many customers don't even bother to receive their items. Please call them once.' He said. 'I'll send you the list.' He stood up. 'These items take a lot of space in the godown.'

'I will make an arrangement.' I assured him.

'I should go now, Ma'am.' He said.

I nodded. He left.

In the evening

'So, how was the day?' Haris was on the call. I was in an auto that refused to run faster. It was already 8 O' Clock in the evening. I waited for an Ola for seventeen minutes and it canceled my ride after that. I was pissed off, but I made peace with my mind and took an auto.

'It was good.' I said. 'I took a decision without informing Dad.'

'What's that?' he asked.

'I called the staff for a meeting tomorrow.' I said. 'I want to know them better and want to talk to them transparently.'

'That's a good idea, Ella. See, how intelligent you are.'

'I have to tell Dad tonight.' I said. 'Plus the godown staff needs increment.'

'I don't think he will oppose it.' he answered for the first sentence. 'Tell your Dad about it.'

'Let's see.'

'What about Kailash? Was he troubling today?'

I chuckled. 'I don't take him seriously anymore.' Haris also laughed at the other end.

'You know what I am starting to like MUSE.' I said finally that I wanted to say since morning.

'Huh...that's the biggest news of the day.' He cheered up.

I smiled. 'But I don't know why.'

'It is a throne of thorns but a throne after all.' I smiled. Haris' sense of humor can beat everything.

'Haris, I want to tell you something.'

'What's wrong?' he sensed the seriousness in my voice.

'Aarav looks exactly like Resham.'

'What?' he laughed. 'Yeah, two people can be lookalikes. So what?'

'It troubles me a lot.'

'Why? It shouldn't. They are a completely different person I believe.'

'Yeah, they are. But whenever I look at Aarav I remember Resham.'

'You had told me that you moved on.'

'Yes, I did.' I said. 'But Aarav looks exactly like him.'

'Oh, Ella!' he probably slapped his forehead. 'You always get into trouble. Now it's emotional. Get out of it, girl. Aarav and Resham are two different people and Aarav is a good person. See how much he supports you. He is the first guy to accept you in the so-called men's world of MUSE. On the other hand, Resham was pure shit. Just get him out of your mind.'

I kept quiet.

'Ella, relax. Whenever you look at Aarav, start thinking about the positive things around you. You can control your mind.'

'I think I can.' I said. 'But it's tough.'

'Go home safely.' He said.

I went home at 9 PM. Dad had called in between. He was naturally worried about me. Though he never shows that.

At the dinner table, I told him about the meeting. He stopped eating. It scared me naturally.

'What will you talk about?' he asked.

'I didn't decide yet. But I think I need to know them properly.'

'So, it will be an introductory meeting?'

'Sort of.' I said.

He resumed eating. I started having my food as well, while Mom and Kaira stared at our faces.

'It's an office, Ella. They are engineers. Your main focus should be extracting their talent. They should get the chance to execute their talents as much as possible. You have to let them work. They should be regular in their work.'

'I understand, Dad.' I said. 'But I think a half an hour meeting won't affect much.'

'I want you to understand the business before doing business.' He said.

'I will keep that in mind, Dad.' I told him about the godown problem. He listened to me carefully and lost in deep thought.

'Dad, are we going on loss?' I asked.

'Not exactly. But things are not smooth. I know that I can't expect things to be smooth in business all the time but this is not what I expect either.'

'Dad, everything will be fine.' I assured him. I went to my room and cuddled with my pillows on the bed. I couldn't sleep well.

iv

'Ma'am, everyone has arrived in the board room.' Aarav said from the door of my cabin.

'Everyone?'

'Yes, Kailash too.' He smiled.

I smiled at his sensitivity. I got up from my chair and took a deep breath, closing my eyes once to imagine the meeting. Nothing much came except darkness. Aarav stared at my face.

'What are you looking at?' I asked him.

'You should not stress much. Everyone is your people.'

'I know but for me everything is new.'

'The company is yours. They are your staff. That's it.'

'You are right, Aarav Shenoy.'

He laughed. I have only seen him laugh aloud thrice, including this one. That's the most critical difference between Resham and him. Resham used to laugh louder all the time.

Resham and I were in a relationship during college. We continued for a year. Things didn't go well because I thought he was stupid. He would crack a joke and laugh at himself. When I told him that he should behave a little mature in public at least, he questioned my love. Okay, I cannot say that I was deeply in love with him, but I shared a good attachment with him. I wanted to continue the relationship and figure something out. He didn't agree much. He decided to break up.

I felt stupid and dejected. I had promised myself that I would never question someone's humor anymore.

'Let's go.' Aarav said in between my guilt trip.

I walked to the board room slowly. I was trying hard to look confident in my blue pants and a white shirt. My Fastrack watch showed 10:58. I was on time and was amazed by the staff as they were on time as well. I felt happy inside that they valued my meeting.

I pushed the door open. The glass door always seems heavy. When I was a schoolgirl, I used to come here often with Dad. Dad always opened the doors for me. I missed Dad.

'Good Morning, Ma'am.' The staff greeted me.

'Good morning.' I replied. 'Please be comfortable.'

I sat in Dad's board room chair. It was very special, and the staff respect the chair very much. My eyes automatically scanned Kailash once. He was wearing a blue T-Shirt on which *"Apna Time Ayega"* was written in bold letters. An excellent choice for T-shirts at the office. I found him scanning me with his sharp eyes as if he wanted to say something.

'Aarav, please take a seat.' I wanted to include him as well.

'Thank you, Ma'am.' He said and took a seat in between Kailash and Ali.

Ali is the senior engineer. Nehal and Kailash work under him as junior engineers. I have heard that Ali doesn't have a degree even. But he is efficient and his degree didn't matter to Dad ever. MUSE was extraordinary just like its staff's choice of clothing at the office. Ali lives in a 2 BHK apartment near the office with his parents. He has a sister who got married a year ago. We were invited to his sister's wedding where Mom and Dad went with 20-gram 22-carat gold earrings. I was amazed by Dad's choice of gift for the staff's sister's wedding. The staff get enough importance from the boss. That is why they are backstabbing by stealing things from the office and selling them outside.

Well, talking about Ali's nature, he is mostly quiet. He greeted me every morning with a sober smile. He is shorter than me in height but elder than me in age. He was twenty-eight. He was in MUSE for three years and did not have a bad record. He respected Dad a lot and gained trust in return. Dad would always talk about his brilliance with a proud voice and sparkling eyes.

Amar is an intern. His internship was for six months. He had joined just a month ago. Amar looked innocent, well mannered, and very young. He was in his final year of engineering and wanted to learn hardware.

'Hello, everyone' I started. 'As you all know, I am very new to this. I am still learning things. However, you are always free to discuss your ideas with me. I'll be glad to listen to your ideas.' I paused. 'Amar, you too.'

'Yes, Ma'am.' Amar responded while the rest of them just nodded.

'Ali, is everything all right at your end? You will report to Dad directly every Saturday as you do. Not to me.'

'Sure.' He said.

'Kailash, Nehal, and Amar will report to me.' I said. 'I'll forward it to Dad.' They nodded.

'Anyone has anything to say?' I asked.

'No, Ma'am.' They all said together.

'Kailash?'

'No.'

'Fine.' I said, 'I have something significant to say.' Every pair of eyes got fixed on my face. I scrutinized all of them one by one. I stood up from my seat.

'I think you all know that our success rate on hardware servicing has decreased. It's 30% lesser than in previous months. Plus, we have lost the customer's assets. The second one is the most important point.' Everyone's body shook a bit. They sat straight. 'MUSE is known for its honesty. It has 20 years of reputation in the market. People trust us. We are losing trust now.'

There was pin-drop silence in the board room.

'There is someone responsible for the loss. I must find out who is behind this.' I said, 'I think you will cooperate with me.'

There was silence again.

'Ali, please focus on the reason of lesser success rate.'

'Sure, Ma'am. There are supplier issues. I don't get required raw materials.'

'That will be fixed soon.' I said. 'Anything more?'

'We have to take more urgent works.'

'Do it.' I said.

'Okay, Ma'am.' Ali responded.

'If needed, work for an extra hour every day. You will be paid for that. And check the jobs of Kailash and Nehal before delivering it to customers. This will decrease the return rate and increase the success rate. And I believe, Amar's work is already checked by Ali.' I said.

Kailash and Nehal were shocked and stared at my face. Aarav licked his lips with his tongue while Amar sat cluelessly.

'Ma'am, we always check properly before delivering.' Kailash snapped.

'Kailash, behave yourself.' Ali said to him.

'That's your job.' I said, turning to Kailash. 'Ali will do his job. Your checking is not enough. If it would, there wouldn't be any return or re-repair.'

They went silent.

'MUSE's success is the responsibility of all of us. I think you get it.' There were low nods.

'Ma'am, we get you completely.' said Ali. 'Don't worry. I'll do my best for the company.'

'Thanks, Ali. Anyone has any question?' There were negative nods.

'Fine. You can go now. Thank you. Have a nice day.' They got up silently and started leaving the room. 'Aarav, stay.' I said.

He had just left his seat but stood beside it. The rest of the staff left. Their facial expression made it clear that they weren't pleased. Except for Ali. He flashed a sober smile at me while leaving.

'That was awesome!' Aarav burst out laughing as soon as the board room evacuated. 'That was so straight forward.' He continued laughing.

'Did I offend them?' I asked softly.

'They are your staff. It's okay, sometimes.' He said. 'It is needed, trust me.'

'Dad never talks to his staff like this.' He nodded in affirmation while I kept quiet.

'But it's okay. It is needed now. You can do it. Sir is very decent and decency doesn't work much in business.' He said, 'Sir told me this only. But he never follows it himself.'

'Dad is very softer inside.' I said. 'I don't think I am like him in this case.'

'That's okay.' He said.

I smiled at him as he stared at me. Haris had said it right that Aarav is very different from Resham.

'What do you think about the lost properties of customers? Who can, possibly, do it?' I said.

'I don't know, Ma'am. I am here for a year now and I don't think anyone of them can do it.'

'Kailash was your school mate right?'

'You know so much.' He said, smiling.

'I didn't decide to sit in this chair just to offend my staff in the early hour of the day. Of course, I did my homework.'

He smiled. 'Yes. He was. And he was not a very brilliant student. He was always bullied by everyone in the school. He was a year senior to me. He can do everything but not steal.'

'Are you sure?'

'I can't be sure. This is business and anything can happen here. He doesn't like you much.' He paused, 'but I don't think he can do it.'

'Who can do it?' I mumbled.

'What about the intern?' he said.

'I don't know.' I said. 'He is very new and a temporary one in the company. He has a motive. He can steal to make some money in six months.'

'I don't think anyone among us can do it.' He said. 'Why would they? They are paid well. They get good treatment here.'

'Let's get back to work.' I addressed him, collecting my stuff. He eyed me all the time, just like I eyed him all the time. I might like him a lot. He is smart and supportive. But he is also an employee of MUSE, and he can manipulate anything in the company. I have to keep an eye on him as well.

Yes, there you go, Ella. Talking like a perfect businesswoman.

I left the board room. Aarav followed me after putting off the ACs.

v

'Hey, how was it?' Haris asked me the first thing as soon as he saw me at his door.

'If you are talking about the meeting, it is not very cool. I tried to be extra bold with the staff.' I answered, throwing my stuff on his sofa. I crashed on the other couch.

He had called me in the afternoon to meet up. As I don't have energy after the office to hang out somewhere else, I decided to land in his flat. Here, I can crash on his sofa comfortably and relax. This was the best place to meet my best friend.

Haris lived alone in the flat. He was trying to transfer his job to the US and settle there for a long time. Even he slept with his previous boss to impress her. But in vain.

'So, what will you have?' He asked.

'*Cutting Chai.*' I said, holding my head.

'Cool. Anything for you, boss.' He giggled. I threw a pillow at him. He caught it with one hand and threw it back at me.

He headed to the kitchen. I got up and went to the bathroom. I looked at my face in the bathroom mirror. I looked pale. Well, just in the first month in MUSE I looked pale to myself. I was exhausted, fully exhausted. I opened the tap and flashed water on my face. I washed my face several times. I tried hard to wash away the dark circles below my eyes. They refused to go anyway. I went to the toilet to pee.

'Are you done?' Haris knocked on the door. 'The tea is ready.'

'I'll not die here. Wait a bit.' I shouted from inside.

'I get tensed. MUSE's new boss' security matters. What if someone pops in from the toilet window and stab you? It happens with business people, you know.'

I opened the door. 'You are reading Agatha Christie and Conan Doyle too much.'

He laughed. 'Thank God, you are safe.'

'Crap. Just drink tea.' We crashed on his sofa again. The clock showed 9 O' Clock.

'I'll drop you home. Have dinner with me, please!' he proposed like every time.

'It will be too late.'

'So what, Aunty and Uncle know that you are here.' He said, sipping his tea, sitting beside me.

'It's not about Mom and Dad. It's about MUSE. I have to get up early, get ready, and run to the office.' I leaned on him and put my head on his shoulder.

He turned to my face. 'Wow!' he finished his tea. I was still sipping and wondering about his "wow". He continued, 'Look at you. Who would believe that this Ella used to miss every Java Programming practical in college for the entire semester just to sleep till 11 AM?'

'People mature up, Haris.' I smiled. I hold my tea with both hands tightly.

'I am surprised. But happy.' He said.

'Many more to come.' I sat up straight. 'You know what Haris, I forgot the last book I read. A person who used to read every day has no relation to the books now.'

'You read "A Walk to Remember", remember? We watched the movie together and you wanted to read the book as well,' he said.

'Yeah.' I nodded. 'You are right. I was reading "A Walk to Remember". You are my best friend, Haris.' I pulled him for a hug. 'I love you a lot.' I almost cried in anticipation. He hugged me tighter.

'Talking about the books, I think I don't have new books to read. We should go to Crossword someday.'

'Order some online, Haris.' I said, releasing him from the most comfortable and asexual hug. 'I can't go anywhere now. I'm busy.' My face hung automatically.

'Buying books online is like eating biryani without that soft potato.' He said.

I laughed. 'If you don't have new books read the old ones. Because reading should not stop.'

'Right you are.' He said, smiling. Then he cleared his throat and asked. 'So what about the lost RAMs?'

'I have to investigate it. It started with RAM...' I sipped my tea, 'next will be a processor...and then a motherboard...a laptop maybe...'

'Think positive.' He said.

'I can't, Haris. Even Dad thinks someone from inside the company did it.' I finished the tea. 'Sudhir told me that he has full faith in the godown boys. They will never do such things.' I paused to put the cup on the table, 'added to it, the things went missing from the office, not the godown.' I left the sofa in anxiety.

'Ella, relax. You'll figure something out. Uncle is still there as the CEO. Don't stress out too much.' Haris pulled me to the sofa again. I sat beside him holding my head.

'C'mon, you are strong, Ella.'

'Hmm, Haris. I am strong. I am bound to be strong all the time.' I said. He pulled me closer for a tight bear hug.

'The tea is good as usual, Haris.' I said, smiling at him. He smiled back.

'Haris, I am pretty sure that it's done by anyone of them only.' I said.

'You are back on the topic again.' He smiled.

I smiled back. 'I am bound to think about it all day.'

'Who do you think can do it?' he asked.

'I doubt Kailash. But Aarav was saying that he can do everything but steal. They were schoolmates.' I said, leaning against the sofa.

'Aarav was in Delhi, right? How...'

'Aarav came back here after his secondary board's exam. He did his higher secondary here.'

'Oh. What about the rest of them?'

'Ali is very professional, he is paid well, and he has, apparently, no reason to steal. That too, just two RAMs.' I said.

'What about the other one, Nehal?'

'I don't know much about Nehal. But according to Dad, he is naive. I don't think he has so much of brain material.' We both chuckled at the end of the sentence.

'But the naive one always does the mishaps.' I added.

'Right.' He said. 'At least detective stories say so.' I gave him a look. He laughed.

'I doubt the intern as well.' I said.

'Aarav can do it as well. He has access to everything, and he knows customers better than anyone.'

'No.' I protested loudly. 'He can't do it, Haris. He's a good guy.' Haris didn't say anything. I found him smiling mischievously.

'What?' I raised my brows.

'You already have a soft corner for him.'

'Shut up, Haris. Will you? He is Dad's secretary. Technically, whoever sits in that cabin, will have him as secretary. I can say that he is the smartest one there. He can never do anything that would ruin his career.'

'I know the look in your eyes, dear.' He laughed. 'You are very protective of him. You talk about him most of the time since you joined MUSE.'

'He's cute.' I said and couldn't stop myself from smiling.

'Oh My God! Ella, what's this?' he teased me, 'already a crush, huh? That too with your assistant!' he continued teasing me.

'Secretary.' I corrected him, smiling.

'It's the same. You are blushing.' He teased me again.

I sat up straight and said, 'Haris, I don't do my staff.' He laughed at that. 'I am serious. I don't like relationships in business.'

'I can sense the odds already.'

'Whatever, Haris, let's have dinner together. See, we didn't have dinner together for so long...'

'Don't try to change the topic.'

'I am not trying to change the topic. I am just hungry.'

Why the fuck I can't stop smiling!

'I caught you,' he laughed again. 'I'm glad to see that you started liking someone again.

'It's just that. Nothing's gonna happen after that.'

'Let's see.' He said.

He ordered dinner on Zomato. I called at home and informed them that I would be late. My parents were not very pleased with that. They wanted me to be back at home and sleep soon so that I don't face trouble getting up in the morning. They were very caring now. Well, they sometimes act more caring than they are expected to be. I hate that for sure but I don't complain.

Sometimes, parents' overaction and extra-care are necessary. That works like a tonic for us, the kids.

'The valet is on the way. He had called.' Haris said, entering the room. He was talking to someone on the balcony. Now I knew that was the valet. I badly wanted him to show up soon. I was hungry like a dinosaur.

'So, coming back to the old topic, you don't like Aarav or hate Resham because they are lookalikes, right?'

'Hell with you.' I left the sofa. Haris was amused. I knew he would tease me with that forever. 'Listen, mister. I give zero fuck about Resham now. And yes, they look alike, but they are very different from each other. Aarav is such a nice kid.'

'Kid?'

'Yeah. He's younger to me, you know.'

'One year younger, dear.'

'Whatever, he's junior. He's my staff. I am his boss. Okay?'

'Okay.' He said in a fake-serious tone. Then he laughed out loud.

'You are an asshole, Haris.'

'You too.' He pulled me closer by my hand. He hugged me the next second. 'I am happy to see you like this. Being at the top of stress level, you never give up. You always find a positive reason to work harder, even in tough situations.' He hugged tighter. I smiled, putting my chin on his shoulder. He continued, 'Aarav is your positivity now. Let's not ruin it.'

He loosened me as the doorbell rang at the same time. It felt hungrier because I knew who it was.

I was happy when I returned home. Haris had dropped me home in his new car. His job was treating him well. His physique had also changed in the last two years. He is fair, tall, and handsome. Yes, he looks better than any other Indian guy. He is four inches taller than me, has deep eyes and a sharp nose.

Before I joined MUSE he was the only guy in my life whose looks inspired me to thank God's creation. Now, Aarav is added to the list. Resham looks like Aarav but I never found him good-looking. Maybe smartness makes you look good, not just your face or body.

Aarav has wide eyes. His brows are brushy and extra curvy. He has a perfect gym-goer's body. He does yoga, he had told me. His lips are maroon and they twitch into a wide smile most of the time. The volume of his hair can drive a woman crazy for sure. They are little curvy on the forehead.

I lay on my bed and stared at the ceiling. If Haris was eight out of ten, Aarav was nine out of ten. He could be ten out of ten as well. Resham was two out of ten. Three points deducted for bad humour and stupidity, three for over-sensitivity, and two for hurting me by breaking up with me.

Was I crazy? I had bigger responsibilities than ranking the boys in my life. I had to find out an imposter who was right in front of me. Who could it be? Kailash? Ali? Nehal? I don't want it to be Aarav.

I was so drained out that night that I don't know when I slept.

vi

Life got busier. One month had passed in MUSE and I didn't even get a trace of the thief. The profit percentage was not satisfactory. Dad's health was under control, but I tried to keep him out of any kind of a mess.

Haris called me several times in the last few weeks. However, we couldn't talk for more than a minute. I worked even after office hours. MUSE was, literally, huge to digest. Even Aarav stayed with me for a few days after office to help me with the junior engineer's accounts. Dad would check it after that. However, I needed to be accurate. I tried my best to impress Dad.

In the process, I fought with Haris one day. He was calling for lunch one Sunday. I rejected his proposal because that is the only day I get some rest. He disconnected the call in anger. I knew that I was going to disappoint a lot of people. I was getting more involved in MUSE and going away from my close ones. For the first time in life, I didn't regret not having friends except for Haris.

I joined MUSE in February. Today was the 6th of March.

'May I come in, Ma'am?' I looked at the cabin's door.

'Come in, Nehal.' I said, putting the accounts file aside. He looked tensed as he wiped out his forehead with a handkerchief.

'What happened?' I asked him. Aarav had left his seat and stood behind me. He also sensed that something was wrong.

'Someone tampered my desktop, Ma'am.' he said, and hesitated a bit before uttering the next sentence, 'and whoever did it wrote some curse words about you as well.'

I jumped out of my chair. 'What's written?' I asked. Nehal kept quiet. I started walking out of the cabin.

'Ma'am, I can't say those words. Please check yourself.' Nehal said, following me. Aarav also walked out of the cabin following us.

I reached Nehal's workspace. The cables were chopped off. The CPU cabinet was on the floor completely broken. Someone had scratched the monitor screen and written something on it. I moved closer and read it.

"Fuck You, Ella! You don't deserve MUSE."

Along with me, Aarav also read it. He stood awestruck, holding his head. Even Nehal was not uttering a word. He lowered his head and stood quietly behind me. My cheeks were hot by now. I was angry. I felt a burning sensation in my ears. I made my hand into a fist and landed it on the table. This shook everyone. Everyone got up from their workspace.

Ali stood up with an air blower in his hand. He was busy working on a motherboard. My eyes went to Kailash. He looked shocked as well. I moved my eyes to Amar. He was clueless, at least his expression said so.

'Who are you?' I shouted at the top of my voice, surprising everyone on the floor. The cleaner, Amod also stopped cleaning the floor and stared at me. 'Who the fuck are you? Come out if you have guts.' I landed another fist on the table.

'Ma'am, stop it. What are you doing?' Aarav instantly caught my fist and stopped me from hurting myself more.

Even in anger, exhaustion, and frustration, I didn't forget to feel his touch. It did something to my body. The hot sensation on my cheeks relaxed a bit. He was still holding my hand tightly. I looked at our hands, and he released it.

'Please, Ma'am, don't do it.' he said softly, in a pleading tone.

I sat on Nehal's chair, holding my head. For a moment, I felt numb. Everything had stopped around me. There was a pin drop silence on the floor. Everybody was still. Only I could hear Nehal opening a bottle and handing it to me. I drank water from the bottle and took a deep breath closing my eyes. I may have reacted more than I should have.

I got up from the seat. 'Listen, guys, I am not here to control you. I am not here to be your boss. Instead, when I came here, I tried to be your friend. I am just trying to fix the issues in the company. I want to save MUSE from going down. If you have any problem with me, talk to me personally. Don't tamper company properties and abuse me. That won't help. That will create bigger problems for you. If MUSE goes down, you all go down.' There was still pin drop silence.

I continued, 'Whoever is doing it you can't be spared from me. I'll catch you one day and that will be the end of your career.' I drank water from Nehal's bottle again. 'I joined MUSE to help my Dad. You know he is not well and he needs me to take care of his hard-earned empire, that is, MUSE. He loves MUSE even more than his family. If you can't accept me, you can't be at MUSE. Because I am not leaving MUSE at any cost no matter how undeserving I am.'

'Whatever is happening, I am sorry for it, Ma'am.' said Ali. 'As a senior staff here, I should have known about it. I am sorry to you on behalf of everyone.

'Why are you sorry if you didn't do anything?' I said. 'I don't understand what's wrong with this company.' I shook my head in disappointment. 'Don't say anything to Dad. Aarav,' I turned to him, 'remove this monitor and throw it in the godown. Fix Nehal's computer. Ali will help you. And again, please don't let Dad know anything about any of these.'

'Okay, Ma'am.' Everyone said in unison.

Nehal's expression made me think. He was the person who broke down the most. He was utterly lost in thought. Maybe it was not a thing to digest for him. Why did his computer tamper? Why not Kailash's? Why not Ali's?

I came back to my cabin. I was alone. Tears rolled down my eyes. What I had thought and what was happening!

Everything went against my expectations. I wanted to make Dad happy. Instead, I have increased my foes.

The telephone rang up. I picked it up instantly.

'Ma'am, Sudhir here. What happened to this desktop? It's completely broken...'

'Someone tampered it, Sudhir. Put it in the godown. We will think about something to do with it later.'

'Things are getting worse, Ma'am. Take action, please.'

'Hmm.' I couldn't utter another word. My throat was jamming, and my eyes turned cloudy. He hung up. I ran to the bathroom to wash my face. Instead, I cried for a minute staring at my reflection in the mirror. 'I don't deserve MUSE?' – my mind repeated the sentence for a long time. I wanted it to be a question only. I didn't want it to turn into a statement someday. I came back to the cabin with a large box of tissues. I sat in my chair and put my head on the table. Aarav was still not back.

'Ma'am.' I heard a voice from the door and lifted my head. Kailash stood at the door.

'Come in.' I said. My voice was still shaking.

'Can I close the door?' he said, holding the latch. I looked at him in shock. This was too much.

'You can trust me. It's for my safety. I have something to tell you that I don't want anyone else to hear. Not even Sir.' I stared at him to sense his motive.

'Please?' he pleaded politely.

When a person completely changes his manner, his voice changes as well. And it changes so much that it makes the person a completely different one. Kailash had never talked to me politely. Today, when he did, I got the shock of my life. But there was more to come.

'Close it.' I said and stayed in my chair, slowly pulling the attached drawer to my table. I placed my hand on tweezers and took it in my hand. I held it in my hand and didn't pull the hand out of the drawer. Self-defence against Kailash was necessary. Tweezers can at least save me from getting raped to some extent.

If the person who wrote those words on the monitor is he, I seriously need a weapon. He locked the door from inside and walked to my table. 'I am... sorry,' he said, hanging his head.

'What for?' I asked.

'I stole those two RAMs and sold it to a customer who buys old stuff and sells them in the black market.'

'I knew it.' I said with a victorious smile on my face.

'Ella, you are intelligent than I thought. I know you have the ability to catch me... I needed money and I couldn't ask for it from anyone as I...'

'...you are egoistic.' I completed the sentence. 'If you ask for money from anyone, it will not be very prestigious for you. So you steal.' He kept quiet, keeping his head down.

'I'm glad that you admit it.' I said.

'I will repay the money to the company.' He said it like he had rehearsed it several times.

'You have to.' I said. I released the tweezers.

'I'm sorry, Ella.' He broke down crying. 'I am very sorry.'

'Kailash, don't cry. Just repay the amount to the company and don't worry. I'll not fire you. Well, I don't have the power to fire anyone. I won't say anything to anyone.'

'Not even Aarav?' he said and it surprised me.

'Not even Aarav.' I said.

'Thank you.' He kept on crying.

There was an awkward silence between us. Kailash stood like a mannequin. I kept on sinking in deep thoughts. I could not disclose this to anyone.

Kailash's career would end forever, and MUSE would carry a bad reputation as well. Most importantly, what would I tell Dad? I was in a deep sea. I had to do something. I had to take action against Kailash so that he would not do it again.

'Who wrote the compliments for me on Nehal's monitor? Who tampered it? You?' It was the best time to question him about everything.

'NO.' He loudly denied. 'I can never write something like that to a woman.' He added, biting his tongue. 'Yes, I was not very happy about your administration in MUSE. I thought you are not sufficient alone. But I cannot do anything more than that.'

'Then who did it?'

'I don't know, Ella.' he folded his hands, 'trust me. I didn't do it.'

'See, Kailash, it's tough to trust you now.' I said. 'Do one thing. Go back to your desk. Do your work. I'll talk to you after office hour.'

'Okay.' He left quickly. But before leaving, he gave me a pleading look. I looked at the clock. It was noon. I had 6 more hours to make a choice for the company. Should Kailash stay or not? Should I say this to Dad? Should I say this to anyone, for that matter?

'Ma'am, May I come in?' It was Aarav now. He was finally back.

'You don't have to take my permission to get in, Aarav.' I said without looking at him.

'Okay.' He said and came by my side. 'Whatever happened there is extremely wrong.'

I smirked. 'Who cares?'

'I do.' He said while getting his hands into work. I stared at his face sometimes. He sensed it after a while and lifted his face to look at me.

'No... I mean, how can somebody be so mean? It's the first time in the office. Someone strictly doesn't want you to be here.'

'Who can it be?'

'Anybody.' He said. 'Anybody at the workplace. I don't trust anyone now. We have a potential rapist in the office.'

'Aarav, this office never had a woman employee. This office never had a woman boss. It's totally a men centric office where people think only men can work. Hardware is not a woman's job. Women are not even worth the deal. And here, I am sitting on this chair, being a woman, is quite unacceptable for them. It hurts so many male egos, you know.'

'You are not wrong.' He said after sometimes. 'But this kind of abusive behavior is not acceptable. You should tell your Dad. And what about your safety?'

'No, Aarav. I have to handle this. It's my test. I have to deal with it. Girls not only need protection from their father, they also need to give protection to their father's empire. This is my test of saving MUSE from the potential rapist you mentioned. And I can protect myself.'

'You are strong and I know you can handle it well.' He smiled finally. 'But you cannot ignore the fact that your father understands these people more than you do. Even more than I do. Maybe he does business in a way different from others, but he ran this company for twenty years.'

I didn't do anything but agree with him.

vii

'Come in.' I saw Kailash appearing on the door. The office was empty now. Only the watchman was there outside, and Amod was cleaning the floor. I could hear his humming of an old Bollywood song in low tune as Kailash opened the glass door of my cabin. He came into the cabin with baby steps. His face was pale as if he had cried a lot.

'Sit.' I showed him the chair in front of me.

'Sorry for everything. Here's the money for the lost items.' He placed an envelope in front of me on the table. Everything happened so quickly that I got confused a bit. I didn't expect him to pay the money today only.

'I don't think I am worthy of this company anymore. I decided to quit.' He said. It was another shock for me. This time also I felt that he had rehearsed the lines.

'But I told you that I'll keep everything a secret. There's no harm for you here.' I told him.

'It's not that. I am not feeling well about myself. I want to quit this job.' He said. 'I thought a lot. I can't continue with such a reputation. Someday people will come to know.'

I kept quiet.

'Ella, madam, I am so sorry.' He added. 'Please release me.'

'Kailash, it's absolutely your choice... but it's not in my hand. Talk to Dad on Saturday. Submit your resignation to him only.'

'What would I do if he asks me the reason of quitting?'

'I can't help you with that either. I don't know.' I said. He nodded.

'You can go.'

He nodded again and walked away. I could see him wiping his tears. I called for a cab and left the office in five minutes. I dialed Mom.

'Ella, where are you? It's so late, beta.' She rattled off on the other side of the phone.

'Yeah, I know Mom. Office stuff, you know.'

'How's your day?' She asked, changing her tone. She was talking like a caring Mom now.

'Adventurous.' I answered.

'Oh, so what did you explore?' she laughed on the call.

'Human nature, Mom.' I laughed back. 'By the way, listen to me, Mom. I am in a cab. I left the office just now. I'm going to Haris' place. I'll stay there tonight. Please manage Dad.'

'Ella, we know that Haris is your best friend and he's a good guy but staying at his place at night...'

'Mom, please. For tonight only. It's important.'

'May I know the reason?'

'No. Just manage Dad, please.'

'Ella, you are so stubborn.'

'I know, Mom. Bye. I'll talk to you later.'

I didn't inform Haris about my visit as I wanted to surprise my best friend, making up for the fight. As I got down from the cab at the gate, the gatekeeper flashed a sober smile at me. He knew me well. I went upstairs.

Haris' flat is the biggest one on the floor. The 3 BHK south-facing flat is located on the 13th floor of the heart of Kolkata. He had bought this flat to live with his parents. But his parents passed away even before he disclosed the news to them. They both passed away from a heart attack in a gap of six months.

Haris was always strong. I didn't see him crying for them. I knew the pain he was suffering inside, but he refused to cry. My friend was good at enjoying life. Haris always gave importance to the present. The past never mattered to him much and he has no time to think about the future.

When you are too busy enjoying the present, you forget the past and don't get time to think about the future. Haris never failed to impress my parents, though.

I reached his flat and pressed the doorbell. He didn't open so I rang the bell again. As I took my phone out to dial him, the door cracked a bit. A face appeared in the dim light.

'Ella!' the voice was familiar but not the environment. I never found his house unlit.

'Haris.' I tried to figure his face out properly. After a few seconds, his face appeared brighter. 'Why is it so dark?'

'It's… umm… well… nothing much. It's just…' his voice hesitated. He was shocked to see me there. I pushed the door to enter the house.

'Ella, how come you are suddenly here?' Haris was still hesitating to let me in while buttoning up his shirt.

'What's wrong? Put the lights on.'

'Who's there?' an unfamiliar female voice filled the house. I followed the voice and got to see a lady silhouette at his bedroom door.

Haris put the lights on. Now I could see a woman wearing an off-shoulder red top and denim shorts. The button of her shorts was open. Maybe she had forgotten to button it up with repeated doorbells. I understood what was happening.

'Ella, she's Manisha. My colleague. We work in the same department.'

The girl was a little uneasy. Haris was hesitant. I never saw him so unprepared in my life. I knew Haris from the ninth standard. He never hides anything from me.

'Hi, Ella.' Manisha waved at me from where she was standing. Her face lit up with a plastic smile. 'Heard a lot about you.'

Haris tried to smile as well but failed.

'Hi.' I said. I could hardly hear my voice.

I looked at Haris, who was still standing by the wall near the switchboard. I was at the entrance of the flat and the girl was at his bedroom door. We were hardly a foot away from each other, but there was a mile's distance between us.

'Ella.' Haris called me. 'Manisha's parents are out of town. So, she stayed here. She doesn't have anyone here.'

'She could have stayed at my place.' I said. 'You could have discussed it with me.'

'No, I mean...'

'What? What do you mean?'

'I didn't want uncle and aunty to get bothered.'

'Oh, really!' I got frustrated, 'Listen, I know what was happening here. You guys are adults and you have full rights to do whatever you were doing here. It's just that I am your best friend, and I deserved to know what's going on in your life.'

'I could say the same as well.' he snapped back. Manisha went back into the room. At least she had some humanity of leaving two best friends alone in a serious talk.

But my friend had lost it downright. He said, 'Do you have time to listen to me? How many times did you call me in the past month? How many times did you call me or meet me since you joined MUSE?' He stood in front of me. Our eyes met. 'Ella, you are too busy to talk to me even. Let alone hanging out.'

'That means you won't tell me that you are dating?'

'I wanted to tell you. It happened just a day ago. And then today her family suddenly left, and she came over. It happened so fast.' He said. 'Why am I explaining it to you?'

'You are acting immature, Haris.'

'Ella, don't act like you are talking to a stranger.'

'A friend who can hide can never be a friend actually, Haris. I know I am busy with MUSE. I know I am trapped with responsibilities. Maybe I am overreacting, but that's the truth of my life now. If that is the reason for our distance, then I can't do anything about it.'

'Fine. Don't do anything. Just handle your business. I can take care of myself. You don't have to come to check on me.'

'Right.' I opened the door to leave. He stood still looking in the opposite direction. 'By the way, have safe sex at least.' I slammed the door behind me. I pressed the switch of the lift. It arrived soon and I went inside, fuming with anger. I cried too.

What was I into? It's all a mess. My staff was against me, Kailash was leaving, somebody was abusing me openly, my best friend was sleeping with a random girl, and I was on the road at 9:30 in the night without knowing what to do.

A month ago, I was a girl who would not get out of home except for work and shopping. Well, I had a job too. But I was an employee then. A month ago, I used to sleep late in the morning and could do anything at any time of the day. A month ago, I was a daughter. Now I was an undeserving boss. My whole lifestyle had changed. It's been just a month and people had a lot of complaints against me.

My phone frightened me in the silence. It was Mom again.

'Did you reach?' She asked as soon as I picked the phone up.

'Yes, Mom.' I said.

'Are you okay?'

'Yes. I'll talk to you later, Mom.'

I don't know if she wanted to say anything more. I disconnected the call.

I was already out of Haris' society. The security guard gave the same smile again. This time, along with curl on his brows. My face muscles tightened enough to not let me smile.

I couldn't go back home now. I couldn't stay on the road either. And I was definitely not going back to Haris' flat. I was thinking about whether I should check into a hotel, my phone's screen flashed with a call that was unexpected at that hour.

'Hello. Aarav. What's wrong?' I was scared by his call at that time of the night.

Was anything wrong in the office?

'Hello, madam. Did you reach home?' he asked, little hesitated.

'Yesss... no... actually, I had come to a friend's home... why?'

'Just asking, Ma'am. Nehal's monitor screen just flashed in my mind. You know the world outside is not exactly a very safe place for a woman at night.'

'Don't take the message on Nehal's monitor screen seriously, Aarav. At least don't go over its literal meaning.'

'So, you are at a friend's place? Please, don't mind. I just wanted to know if you reach safely.'

'Aarav, I think you have the spare key to the office.' The bulb in my head lit up.

'Yes, Ma'am. Why?' his voice slowed down a bit.

'Actually, I need the couch to sleep.'

'Huh? What are you saying?' Aarav was confused.

'I am saying that I need the key. I am coming to your place, just come down of your building and give me the key.'

'But why do you need the key at this hour, Ma'am?' he said, 'It's almost 10 PM.'

'Aarav, I'll tell you later. Just give me the key. Where do you live in Elliot Road?'

'But Ma'am...'

'WhatsApp me the address.' I disconnected the call and took a taxi.

'Elliot Road.' I told the driver.

My phone beeped. I read the address to the driver. He nodded in affirmation. My wristwatch showed 9:55 PM. I stared at the road. Everyone was busy even at this hour of the day. Why don't people take a break?

The taxi entered Park Street. Momentarily, I could see dark graves from the gap of the green-colored gate of the South Park Street Cemetery. I imagined mysterious creatures busy in their schedule. Because I don't think even ghosts have time to sleep in this city. Maybe some ghost's friend betrayed her, and she was heading towards an official grave to spend the night. Who knows? Even spirits can have life.

In a few minutes, I reached my destination. The building where Aarav lives weren't in excellent condition as it's one of the oldest constructions on Elliot Road, I suppose.

We saw each other at the same time. He was wearing a black T-Shirt and black track pants. His slippers shined in the street light. It was probably newer than the rest of the things he was wearing.

'I am confused. You said you are in a friend's house.' He said, coming close.

I said, 'I had come to a friend's house.' I cleared it out for him, smiling. I paid the driver and turned to him. The vehicle left and it felt like I was alone with him.

'What happened? You don't look good.' He said.

'I am trying to look good.' I said. 'But I am failing, constantly, you know.'

'What happened, Ma'am? You are scaring me. I am already scared after reading that message on Nehal's monitor.'

'Well,' I lowered my voice, 'I am homeless for the night. I went to my best friend's house to have a friendly and relaxing late-night chat, games, and whatnot. Instead, I found him with a random girl whom he introduces as his girlfriend. I left his flat obviously and he did not stop me.' I took a deep breath.

'So? Why didn't you go back home?'

'I already told my parents that I am going to Haris' place and I don't want my parents to hate him.'

'But he deserves hatred.' He said. 'How can he slee… I mean, spend the night with a random girl, and most importantly, how can he leave you alone at night?'

'He's angry with me.' I said. 'For the past few days, we didn't talk like before. I couldn't keep my focus on him.'

'He should understand that you are at MUSE now and it's not his 9 to 5 corporate job.'

'How come you know about his job?'

'I heard you talk to him at the office.'

'Aarav!' Loud laughter escaped my mouth. 'You spy on me.'

'No. I just do my job. Keeping my sense organs active.'

'You are funny.'

'And you are scary, seriously, Ma'am.'

'Give me the keys.' I said. 'I have to call a cab or taxi again.'

'You are going to sleep in the office?'

'Yes. And nobody should know about it except you. Not even your girlfriend or anyone.'

'I don't have a girlfriend.' He loudly protested as if I have accused him of keeping illegal weapons.

I chuckled.

'I am serious, Ma'am.'

I smiled, looking at my phone. Well, who didn't want him to be single?

'Okay, I got the cab.'

'You can't open the locks alone. Plus you don't even know the meter room. You won't get electricity supply.' He said. 'Most importantly, it's not safe for you to stay alone there at night.'

'So? Tell me how to open the locks and where the meter room is. And don't worry about my safety. I have pepper powder and sharp tweezers in my pocket.' I slapped my jeans' left pocket. For a moment, his eyes got fixed in my pocket.

'Please, go back home, Ma'am.' He said. 'It's stupidity to sleep at the office.'

'Are you calling me stupid?'

'No.' He said, 'Sorry, I didn't mean it like that.'

'Okay, apology accepted.'

'What will Sir think if he comes to know?'

'He will come to know only if you tell him.'

'I won't tell him.' He said. 'But if you go there alone, people will get to know. Ma'am, it's an office, and you can't open it at this hour. Local people will not see it justified.'

'You are too complicated, Aarav.'

'Maybe Ma'am. But I can't let you go there alone. I'll go with you, please wait here.'

'What?' he already entered the old gate of his building, 'Aarav at least give me the keys.' I roared.

'Give me a minute. I'll just change and come.' He shouted back.

'You have three minutes to get ready.' I said again. He just waved while approaching the staircase.

From where I stood, I could see no sign of lift in the building. I don't know on which floor he exactly lives. I waited for the cab down. It was 2 minutes away by now.

viii

'Ma'am, we can't let anybody see us opening the office at this hour.' Aarav whispered at me in the cab.

'Okay.' I said.

'Did you have dinner?' he asked.

'No.' I said. 'You?'

'Not yet. I told Mom that my friend got stuck in the station. I have to fetch him to a hotel. I had to lie.'

'I didn't ask you to lie. I didn't ask you to come with me at all.' I snapped.

'I didn't say it like that.' He said. 'Well, we almost reached. I think we should buy something for us to eat. We can get it packed.' He said.

I nodded in affirmation. Well, I was hungry like a maniac. It's just that I had to forget about it. But now I remember that I have a stomach and it was aching with hunger.

Aarav could actually change in just three minutes. He was now wearing black jeans and a dark blue shirt. His feet now had a sneaker. He looked handsome. He was seated in the front passenger seat, and I was at the back. What was he up to? Was he planning to spend the night with me at the office? That would be too much for a day to take in. And if Dad comes to know about this part especially, I have to forget about MUSE forever. Well, I was in too much risky business. The cab dropped us in front of the office gate.

'Do you have a problem with street food?' he asked me.

'Not at all.' I said.

'Okay.' I followed his eyes. He was eyeing a street stall across the road which was about to close.

'Let's see what we get there.' I told him, paying the cab.

We reached the stall that was staffed by a lady in black saree. A man was putting the dishes into a large tin container. They were probably getting ready to leave.

'Mashi, what's there?' I asked.

'Only *naan roti* and chicken.' She said, smiling.

'Pack for two.' I said. 'How much?'

'One hundred and twenty rupees.' She said, and I took out my purse.

'Thank God at least food doesn't cost much.' I whispered to Aarav.

'You should not eat chicken. They don't clear and cook properly.'

'Shut up.' I laughed. 'Don't talk like my father.'

'Okay.'

Then we burst out laughing on the road.

The woman packed the food by then. I handed her a blue-colored new 100 rupee note and two ten rupee coins.' She took it with a smile.

'You are MUSE *wali didi*, right?' the man asked from behind. I didn't notice when he came behind us.

'Huh?'

'Yes, I know you.' He said, smiling.

'Yeah. We have some work here. So...'

'*Haan haan samjha, didi. Aplog ka kam hi toh aisa hai.* You often come at night.'

I didn't take his statement seriously that night. Otherwise, I would have known a lot of things at that moment.

'*Haan ji.*' I took the food packet swiftly and left the stall.

'If he tells anything to Sir any day, I am fired.' Aarav whispered to me.

'Stop whispering like that.' I scolded him. 'He won't say. Why would he?'

'This is India. People love being RAW agents.'

'Shut your poor jokes up.'

He just giggled.

We approached the gate. We looked at the stall at the same time.

'Let them go.' I said. He nodded.

The man was loading a tempo. The woman was switching off the lights. The man now pulled the hoarding down. Hoarding that has all kind of pictures of different food items available there. "Fresh Food and Beverage Centre" was written on yellow hoarding with red ink.

They didn't even look at us once. We were standing in front of our office gate. It's usually dark at this side. And with their lights off, now we were in a darker zone. So, less chance for anyone to notice us. They finally left.

'Let's get in.' Aarav spoke up.

He started unlocking each one of the seven locks. They were huge combination locks. He opened them very carefully while making minimum noise.

'I never thought that I have to sneak in my own office like this.' I said.

'Isn't that enough for your adventurous mind?' he said smirking.

'How did you know I love adventure?' I asked.

'I saw you reading Harry Potter and Agatha Christie. Even you read Satyajit Ray. I saw you reading Feluda Series in Bengali.'

'Oh well. I love reading adventurous and mystery books.' I replied, smiling. 'And I know Bengali. But for a long time, I didn't read a single book.' I said sadly.

'I also read Bengali.' He said.

'Really?'

'Yes. I had a Bengali friend in Delhi. She taught me.'

'That's cool.' I was more than happy to know about his skills.

'Will you light the torch on your phone for me?' he said while trying to lock the gates from inside.

Once the shutter was pulled down, it was utter dark inside.

'Wait, let me light the torch first. It's too dark here.' I shouted.

'It's okay I can see, but for your safety light the torch.'

'You just asked me to light the torch for you.' I said.

'Light it, please, Ma'am.' He laughed.

I lit the torch finally. He started locking. We headed inside and he went towards the meter room. I kept my torch lit. Aarav walked ahead of me. We finally reached under the ground floor's staircase.

'Watch your steps.' He said and crawled under the staircase to open a wooden cabinet. He started pulling the switches up.

One. Two. Three. Four. After pulling up four switches, the office became fully visible. All the lights and fans and ACs were on.

'Okay, now as we don't need all of them, light only the necessary ones.' He said.

'Hmm.'

'Are you okay?' he said.

'I am starving.' I said in a plain voice.

'Let's go to your cabin.'

I started climbing the staircase already. I rushed into my cabin. He switched off all the unwanted lights, fans and ACs and came into my cabin, and set the temperature of the AC. By now, Aarav had known everything about my habits. He put a freshwater bottle on my table that he probably grabbed from the pantry while coming upstairs. He also spread a newspaper on the table for me to eat.

'You should get the best employee's award.'

'Are you starting something like that?' he laughed.

'I mean why not if there's deserving employee's like you?'

'And for what I should be awarded? For spreading the newspaper on the table or for sneaking into the office with my boss' daughter at 10.30 pm?'

I looked at his face. 'I didn't call you here.'

'I know.' He said, sitting on the chair in front of me. 'I didn't mean it like that.'

'You should be awarded for understanding me and accompanying me when I needed a company.'

He smiled. 'That's my responsibility. Sir gave me life when I was nothing. I learned everything from him. I learned to be a good human from him only. Nobody showed me so many sides of life as he did. I didn't get my father's company much. Sir is like a father figure to me.'

'Dad is very peculiar. I want to be like him.'

'You are an amazing daughter, Ma'am. I have never seen one like you.'

'And what I am exactly?' I said while putting *naans* in my mouth like a hungry dog. I was shameless while eating. He too started eating his share.

'You can't be expressed in a few sentences, Ma'am.' He said. 'I should get a glass for you.' He left the chair in the next second. I wanted him to finish his food first. But he was already out of my sight.

I smiled while he left the cabin. Something was there in this guy that made me feel safe that night. He impressed me day by day and was making me forget Resham and his crazy acts. It was like Aarav was putting everything in the right order for me. Suddenly, my life was experiencing a different adventure!

'Here's the glass, Ma'am.' He put the glass on the table. I didn't notice when he came inside.

'Thanks.' I said, and don't call me Ma'am after office hour, please.'

He stared at my face.

'I don't like it. Call me Ella.'

He laughed.

'What happened?'

'I am not habituated with calling my boss by name.'

'I am not exactly your boss. Also, I am not old enough to be called ma'am all the time. Not at least after office hours. If you can't call me with my nickname "Ella" then you can call me by my real name.'

'Even your nickname is awesome.' He said.

'Yeah, not very bad.'

'At least better than mine.' He said, getting up from the chair.

'What's yours?'

'You wouldn't want to know that.' He chuckled.

'You will sleep on the couch, your special couch,' he said while pointing towards the couch beside him. 'I'll lie on the bench in the workspace.'

'No.' I protested. He gave me an indifferent look.

'I mean, you came here to accompany me, right? Bring the bench here. You can share this corner, and I can lay on that corner, on the couch.'

He stared at my face sometimes. He was expressionless. Was I trying to be too bold? Ghosshhh! It's bad.

'Okay.' He gently said, and left the cabin.

I washed my hands, got freshen up in the bathroom, and came back in the cabin. Aarav was back by then with the bench. He put it in the opposite corner to the couch and sat on it. I sat on the couch. The big working table stood like a wall between us. I laid down.

'Put the lights off, Aarav.' I said.

'Huh?'

'Just put the lights off. I can't sleep until its complete dark.'

'Okay.' A nervous reply came following slow footsteps. The light went off with a click of the switch.

I smiled in the moonlit room.

'Is it a full moon?' I asked.

'Umm... most probably, Ma'am.'

'Call me Ella.'

'Okay.'

The bench creaked a bit. I assumed that he laid down on it. He had brought cushions from someone's chair. We made it our pillows.

Along with the light of the moon, cold air gushed inside the cabin from the open window.

'Are you comfortable?' I asked.

'Yes, Ma'am.' came the reply. 'Sorry, Ella.'

'Better.'

'You didn't tell me your nickname.'

He laughed. 'You are very stubborn.'

'I know.'

'Ballu.' He said, laughing.

'What?' I sat up laughing. 'Ballu? What kind of a name it is?' I continued to laugh my lungs out.

'Some uncle of mine had started calling me with that weird name.' He said.

'He fucked your name totally.' I choked laughing.

'He did. Are you okay?'

'Yes.' I replied, laughing. 'It's horrible. I want to forget this conversation. Whenever I imagine you as "Ballu", I see the furry and goofy version of you.'

'Stop imagining then.' He also laughed.

'Aarav, what was your aim in life? Nobody aims to become a secretary.' I asked, changing the topic.

'You are right. Nobody does.' He said. 'I wanted to do an MBA after graduation and set my own business up. But for now... I am in MUSE.'

'I forgot my aim, Aarav. What I wanted to be, doesn't matter anymore. What I want to be, I can't figure out now.'

'Everything will be fine, Ella. Sometimes, you achieve more by going against your aim.' He said in an assuring tone.

'Good night.' I said.

'Good night, Ella. Please sleep.'

'You too.'

The bench creaked again. I could figure his body move as he probably turned towards the wall.

What a day! The way it started and the way it ended both I'll remember forever. I never had a day like this. Was it a good one? Or a bad one? No, not a bad one, I am sure.

ix

'Dad, why don't we set up CCTV cameras in the office?' I asked Dad the next day at the dinner table.

He smiled while eating. 'If we do, the staff will consider that we are monitoring them all the while. They will think that we have put them in the cage.'

'Dad, even small companies have CCTV cameras.'

'I know, Ella. But it's not something I like to do. I don't want to keep an eye on my staff all the time. They should be given freedom at least during their work.'

'We can put a camera at the entrance.' I said.

'What happened, Ella?' He stopped eating. 'Is there any problem? Why are you forcing me to deploy cameras?'

'Dad, we could have known the RAM thief or smuggler, whatever you like to call him if we had cameras.'

'When you put cameras to monitor, they are afraid of the cameras, not you. Staff will do their job just like the lion jumps over the fire due to the fear of the stick in the circus. They will not work with their heart. They will work out of fear.'

It was not possible to win over Dad. He would always prepare an answer ready for my next question. I don't think he was wrong that day. He was right in every way.

'I am thinking of godown staff's increment in the next month.' Dad said when I didn't say anything after a long time.

'Can we afford it?' I asked.

'Not exactly. But the staff's happiness is also important. If they are not satisfied with the salary, they will not focus on the work and will always think that they deserve better than what they are getting.'

I nodded, agreeing.

On Friday, the 8th of March, Dad returned home with a very serious face. He went to the office and came back after me in his car. He wanted to take me home with him but I refused as I wanted to go home with Aarav. We went together in the same cab, and I dropped him in his house.

'What happened in the office?' Dad asked me after returning after two hours.

'Nothing.' I said softly. 'Anything wrong, Dad?' My heart started beating faster. I sensed the tension in Dad's face.

'Kailash suddenly came up with a resignation letter in the evening after you left. What's wrong in the office?'

'What did he say?' I asked while trying to act normal.

'He didn't provide any valid reason in the resignation letter. I cannot ask even. This is not the Kailash I know. Did he say anything to you? Did he speak of any problem in the office?'

'No, Dad.' I swallowed a lump of saliva down.

'Are you the problem?' Dad almost talked to himself.

I was near to a more certain cardiac attack.

'Dad,' I called out. 'Please sit.' I showed the sofa to him. He sat, staring at my face. I sat beside him.

'Dad, I think Kailash doesn't like me. Or there is someone else who doesn't like me there.'

'So what? He will resign?' he got disturbed. 'This is so childish. He is breaking his own legs by leaving the job. Doesn't he know that?'

'I don't know the exact reason, Dad. But this can be a reason.' I said, hiding a lot of things.

He kept quiet sometimes and started rubbing his hands with each other. His forehead got some uneven curls as he drank two sips of water from the bottle itself. I kept seated like before. I waited for Dad to speak out.

'What should we do?'

'Huh, Dad?'

Was he seriously asking me this?

'What would you do if you were in my place?' Dad asked, looking straight at my eyes.

'I...' I looked down, then at him, again down, 'well, I would let him go. I don't have any rights to stop him from doing whatever he is doing.'

Dad kept quiet.

'Dad, we can hire someone in his place. The company will not face any serious problem, I guess. You always know better than me but what I know is MUSE is not dependent on anyone or anything. It's the most independent company I have ever seen.'

'His notice period starts from tomorrow. 9th of March. Should I approve of it?' Dad asked me.

'I think you should.' I said.

Dad kept quiet. He kept seated on the sofa. I got up and went to my sister's room. Kaira was studying. She looked at me from the study table.

'Hey.' She whispered at me.

'Hey.' I said, crashing on the bed. I stared at the ceiling. Precisely, at the ceiling fan.

'What happened?' she continued whispering.

'Kailash wants to resign. Dad is confused naturally as this is sudden. I convinced him to grant his resignation.'

'Oh. Kailash is the rough and tough guy, right?' she tried to remember him.

'Yes. The one who hates me from the very beginning.' I whispered almost to myself.

'The company is yours. Not his.' She said. 'Let him go.'

'You know what, Kaira.' I got up. She turned her chair to me. 'Something is fishy.'

'Where?' she asked.

'There. There, in the resignation letter.'

'What's that?'

'Kailash didn't provide any valid reason. Plus he's paid well. He and Nehal work in the same position. Still, he's paid more than Nehal. They joined together, but Dad did Kailash's increment recently. Then why the fuck he wants to resign?'

'Because of you, maybe?' she hesitated to say this but finally said.

'I don't think so. Somebody doesn't leave a good job because of a silly reason like this. I don't think Kailash is the person he looks from outside. There's something fishy going on. I need to find it out.' She stared at my face. I left the bed.

'Kailash is guilty of stealing those two RAMs. Don't tell anyone.' I said as soon as I saw her face changing color in shock. 'Yes, he confessed about it. He paid for the RAMs as well. And just then he declared his resignation to me. Today he submitted the resignation letter to Dad.'

'When did he confess?'

'Day before yesterday.' I said. 'He was giving me the resignation letter but I had asked him to deal it with Dad.'

'So, you think all these are fishy?'

'Yes. The RAM's matter was solved. I forgave him and promised that I won't say this to Dad or anyone in the office. I kept my promise but he wants to leave. That's where I think something's wrong. He's hiding something. When he was confessing to me, I felt that he came after proper rehearsal.'

'So, what's next?'

'Investigation.' I hold her chair from the back. 'I have to investigate it.' She turned to me, confused, I continued holding the chair and looking blankly at the wall, 'I need a Watson for this.'

'And who can it be?' she asked, getting up. Her eyes lit up behind the thick glass she was wearing. She was amused. Her lips twitched to a funny shape. It's extra curvy now.

I smiled. 'I know who it can be, sister. You will come to know everything, dear.' I patted her shoulder and came back on the bed. 'You better keep your mouth shut regarding all these and focus on your masters.'

'Yeah yeah.' She sat on the chair again. 'But Kailash is leaving. How will you investigate?'

'I have 15 days for that.' I said. 'It's Kailash's notice period and my time to create history.'

'Yeah. Fine. All the best. And if possible let me know who the Watson is.'

'Aarav.' I said, smiling.

'If something's fishy with Kailash, then something is roasting between Aarav and you. I can sense that. You talk about him so much.'

'Whatever.' I couldn't stop smiling.

'By the way, Haris has called me in the morning. He was saying that you blocked him on WhatsApp and Facebook.'

'Yes, I did. He deserves it. Tell him to screw his new chick.'

'You guys will never stop fighting like this.' She laughed.

'I can forgive him only if he falls on my feet.' I said, 'let him know this.'

'Okay.' She chuckled.

Well, I was really very angry with Haris when I left his house. But then you know what happened. I spent the most beautiful time of my life with a guy I liked, just because of the thing that happened with Haris. So, I technically forgot about the negative stuff. It's quite right that I try to find out the positive things even out of negative ones very easily.

For now, I had to focus on being Sherlock. Everybody doesn't get a chance like this. It may be one chance in a lifetime for me. I had to start my investigation. I told Aarav to meet me. As it was Sunday, we planned to meet outside. He had asked me the reason for this meeting. I didn't disclose anything to him, though.

I informed Kaira about our meeting outside the office for the first time. Kaira looked at me from the corner of her eyes. I saw this and turned towards the wall, smiling.

'For the first time, Sherlock is falling in love with her Watson.' She said screwing the Maggi noodles in a fork.

'Shut the fuck up, please!' I protested. 'I don't like relationships in business.'

She continued laughing hysterically as if I cracked a joke.

x

Sunday Morning

'Happy belated Women's Day.' The screen of my phone flashed with a notification from my best friend. I had unblocked him last night on WhatsApp.

'Doesn't suit you.' I replied.

'Unblock me, please. I can explain it.' His message popped in.

I unblocked him on call.

'Ella, breakfast is ready.' Mom called from the door.

Kaira was still sleeping like *Kumbhkarn* in her room. Our rooms face each other and I can see her from my bed.

'Coming, Mom.' I said.

My phone rang up. Haris was calling.

'*Bol chutiye.*' I didn't find a better word for him.

'Okay, first of all, thanks for unblocking me. Secondly, sorry for that night. I owe you an explanation, but you are also not a fresh butt. Okay?'

'Ohkay.' I said, 'I am the worst. But that night I didn't expect you to screw a random girl and lie about it.'

'Which lie are you talking about?'

'She's not your girlfriend. She's just a random girl from your office or maybe a red light girl.'

'What the fuck!'

'What?'

'She's my girlfriend.' He said. 'But yes, I'm not sure about her. Not even after sex. She's quite moody. She says she loves me but can't commit. I slept with her because she has a good relationship with the boss. So, maybe she can help me in... you know.'

'Stop screwing her.'

'I'm thinking of what to do. I wanted to talk to you regarding this for a few days. But you, an asshole, didn't pick my call up.'

'I am sorry for that. I was busy. Things are getting crazy at MUSE.'

'Now what happened?'

'I'll tell you later. I am at home and it is not the right place to spit about the crazy things.'

'Oh, well.' He said. 'Then meet me in the evening. We can discuss everything in detail.'

'I can't. Not today. I can meet you tomorrow after the office.' I said.

He kept quiet.

'I have something important to do regarding MUSE. Sorry for avoiding you again. Please don't sleep with a random girl for this now.'

'Shut up, *chutiye.*'

'You shut up, Haris. You are such a bad friend.'

'By the way,' he said as if he recalled something suddenly, 'that night you didn't go home. Kaira told me. Where were you?'

'That's none of your business.' I whispered.

'Why are you whispering?' he said. 'I told Kaira that you left that day at night only. She was shocked and told me that you didn't come home.'

'I was at the office.' I made my voice as low as possible.

'What? I didn't hear you.' He shouted.

'I was at MUSE.' I said softly again.

'What? Alone?' Now he heard me finally.

'No. Not alone. I don't have the keys.'

'Aarav was there.' He said. 'I knew it. I knew you were with him only. You can spend the night with a random guy but I can't. Wow, well played, you hypocrite.'

'Hey, mind your language, brat! He is not a random guy. And we were not making out, yuck, I can't even think about it. We slept at different corners.'

'Who will trust you?' his voice had apparent mischief.

'We don't care about anybody.' I said.

'Oh well, the boss and the staff are on the same team now. Poor Dad of yours! Doesn't know what's going on behind his back.'

'Chup hoja, Kutte.'

He laughed wholeheartedly as if I complimented him. 'Okay, tomorrow at my home. And if in case you cancel it I will sleep with Manisha again.'

'Fuck you!'

'With pleasure.'

'Ella, breakfast is getting cold. Don't eat. Only sleep and talk on the phone.' This one came from the kitchen. It was loud enough for people on Mars to hear.

I disconnected the call and left the bed. I found Kaira in my room.

'So you two spent the night together...?' she giggled. 'That's awesome. I would like to meet him someday. Or soon?' she yawned.

'What are you doing here? And we didn't sleep together.'

'You are turning red.' She said.

'Let's have breakfast. Mom is calling for breakfast since forever. C'mon.' She giggled.

I left the room while trying hard to look normal. Kaira followed me. We struggled to brush our teeth together in the same mirror. She pushed me, and I elbowed her. We finally joined Mom and Dad at the breakfast table at 8:30 AM.

'By the way, Mom, I'll be going out for a few hours in the evening.' I said while eating bread toast.

'Any plan with friends?' Mom asked. Dad also gave a questioning look. Kaira chuckled, almost choking on the milk.

'No.' I tried to act normal again, 'I mean, yes. I am going out with some ex-colleagues. It's a small get-together.'

'Okay. But return soon. Tomorrow you have...'

'I know, Mom.' I smiled.

'Yes, tomorrow you have special tasks to do...'

'You please, stop pulling my legs.' I cut off Kaira.

I got ready by 3:30 PM. I had to take a cab to Elliot Road to pick up Aarav. I booked an Ola.

'I have a gift for you.' Kaira announced just before I leave home.

'Oh, really!' I got excited. 'Why didn't you tell me before?' I sat on the bed.

'Okay. It's a surprise, so I wanted to gift it to you now. This is the best time for gifting people on women's day according to astrology.'

I stared at her face with awe. 'Women's day is over. You are a shit.'

She laughed and took out a big brown envelope from under the mattress of my bed. I checked my phone for the cab. Five minutes left for the cab to arrive. She pulled out a big poster-size paper from the envelope.

'Here, your women's day gift. Every woman needs a positive influence to do whatever she's dreamt of doing. Here's your positive energy.' She announced.

I was clueless about the gift. I could only see the white back of the poster. I took it from her. Her face was refusing to stop laughing and giggling. Something was fishy for sure.

I turned the poster. I was shocked. My forehead got curls for sure though I couldn't see my own face.

'It's Resha... No.. Aarav.' I looked at her, 'What the fuck! It's Aarav's portrait!'

She laughed loudly. 'Your positive inspiration.'

'You are a fucking asshole.' I said, but I couldn't stop admiring the portrait. 'Who made this?' I asked.

'An App in my phone has the feature of turning any photo to sketch. I used it. I downloaded his picture from Facebook.' She said.

'He's on Facebook?' I questioned.

'Yes. I thought you know it.'

'No. I don't know.'

'Okay,' she said, 'I'll suggest you.'

'No need of that.' I said. 'I can find him out myself.'

'That's cool. How's the gift?'

'Little risky.' I winked at her.

My phone rang. The driver called. He had reached the location.

'Well, try not to exhibit it to Mom and Dad. Don't burn my ass. Hide the poster, you fucking asshole.' I smiled at her.

'Don't worry.' She laughed, taking the poster from me. I proceeded towards the main gate. 'Mom and Dad, I'm leaving.'

'Okay, Ella. Come back soon.' Mom said.

Dad was sleeping most probably as he didn't respond. We didn't have any talk about Kailash since the last evening. I knew Dad would do the best. He understands business more than anyone associated with MUSE does. He's a genius businessman. I admire Dad in every field of my life. I always wanted to live life and not just breathe. Dad also had the same motto when he was of my age.

Dad and I share several similar interests. He's funny, jolly, and sarcastic and has a remarkable sense of humor. People say I also pose these characters. Dad and I both are a special kind of an introvert.

Well, in my opinion, there are two types of introverts - "pure" and "mixed". The pure introvert is the shy one and does not want to talk to people that much, not even in need. They are basically afraid of talking to random people. They will not eat for a day but won't receive the delivery boy's call just to confirm the address. The mixed introvert is a kind of mixed breed that have some qualities of an introvert and some of the extrovert. They are the most interesting ones in the world. They are dynamic as well. They do not talk much but when they talk, they engage everyone around them. People generally like them. But when people hate them, they continue hating them for a long time.

Dad and I belong to this "mixed introvert" breed. Interesting, isn't it?

That's where the clue of the case laid. Kailash hated me from the very beginning. But suddenly he confessed everything to me and became a very good person. And then he resigned. If he hated me, he should always hate me, just like the case of Aarav. He likes me from the very beginning. He didn't change. Why did Kailash change? He didn't bang his head and change, I suppose!

The car suddenly took a left turn. I was almost banging my head on the front seat. Well, I escaped from a narrow 'bang'.

xi

'Hey. Happy Sunday!' Aarav waved at me while getting in the cab.

'Happy Sunday!' I said, smiling. 'I spoil your holiday.'

He smiled.

He looks better than the portrait.

'Where are we going?' he inquired from the passenger seat.

'We are going to the highway.'

'Why?'

'We need privacy.'

'Wh..at?'

'I mean we need to discuss something secret. We can't let a creature know about it.'

'What's so secret?' his eyes were blank.

'It's about MUSE.' I said.

'Hmm.' He said.

I nodded. We crossed the Second Hoogly Bridge in a few minutes. There's no traffic on a Sunday. Though sometimes traffic in Kolkata is more disappointing than the traffic in Bangalore and Mumbai. The cab dropped us at the highway. We went inside Cafe Highway and settled ourselves.

'So, what's the matter?' he asked me after taking a quick look at the menu card.

'Do you think Kailash can steal?' I asked.

'You already asked me this. And I had an answer for this.' He said. 'Can I order coffee for us?'

'I don't drink coffee.' I said. 'If I say Kailash stole those two RAMs and sold it in the black market, is it very hard to believe?'

His jaw dropped. He was shocked and dropped the menu card on the table that made a low thud upon dropping.

'Kailash can never do it.'

'Is it tough to believe that he confessed everything and resigned on the same day?'

'YES!' he shouted, 'What the f... Sorry. He resigned?'

'How can you be so sure?'

'I have proof.' He said, hovering over the table to come close to me.

'What proof?' I asked in the same way.

'Madam, anything?' the waiter asked us now. We didn't order anything till then.

'Yes.' Aarav spoke up before I could say anything. 'One coffee and one tea.'

'Big or small?'

'Big.' I said.

'I'm paying for this.' Aarav whispered to me.

'Why?'

'My wish.' He said almost like a command.

I didn't drag the conversation more. I just smiled.

He stated, 'The day all these happened, Kailash was absent. In fact, he was on leave to visit his hometown.' I was dumbstruck. 'From the very beginning, I knew he didn't do it.' he continued. 'There's someone who's doing it. Something is not right. This job is his last hope. Why would he resign? And if he wanted to resign, he could have done so right away. Why did he confess and resigned?'

'My questions are the same.' I said. 'I also think something's fishy.'

'Yes, there is something fishy. So what do we do now? You didn't call me here to drink coffee only, I suppose?'

'You have to be my Watson.'

'You are Sherlock?'

I looked at his sheepish expression. He burst out laughing. The people from other tables looked at us, probably considering us to be a crazy couple. I wish!

'Behave yourself.' I said, laughing. 'You are not supposed to laugh at your boss' decision.'

'Oh, really? But I think we are outside the office and you are Sherlock, and I am Watson. Sherlock doesn't behave like this with his friend.'

'Hmm.' Aarav had a kid inside. Well, what could I expect more from a 23-years-old guy?

The tea arrived. It was smocking hot. I felt the smoke coming out of hot terracotta mugs. He took his coffee mug and sipped it hot.

'The smell is amazing. Cheers to our new mission.' He took another sip of the coffee.

'Cheers to our newly formed friendship.' I said.

He just smiled very cutely looking at me for a brief second.

Did you ever see a person smile from inside? Where his face glorifies and eyes talk a lot. Where his nose swells up in excitement and lips perched on each other to hold the smile. Where his forehead gets curves and cheeks get burned with redness. Aarav's smile was something like that only. It escaped from him and dissolved in me. For months I couldn't forget that smile. Except for Haris, I never had a good friend. I fight so much with Haris but he comes back every time. We have a different understanding where we love to be with each other no matter what.

When I met Resham, I had thought that he could be my good friend and he would understand me as Haris do. But no, he was very different.

And now when I was sitting in this cafe with my secretary, with my Watson, with a new friend, or whatever he meant to me, I feel complete. Right at that moment, I realized one thing very clearly. I liked Aarav! I knew the next thing as well. We couldn't get along. The reasons were many...

I met Aarav's mom that evening. He insisted me to go to his home and meet his mother. She was a lady in her mid-fifties. She has dark brown eyes and a wheatish complexion. Her eyes had dark circles and lips were dried up - probably from the high dose of medicines.

She was delighted to see me, and she was not pretending. She made me sit on a small sofa and sat beside me.

I scanned Aarav's flat. It was an old building, as I predicted earlier. There were two small rooms and a kitchen and a bathroom. The place where I was sitting was an open space that they use as a drawing-room. There was a small sofa, a refrigerator, an old grandfather clock, and a small wardrobe. A wooden table was placed in front of the sofa. I could see the kitchen that was small but well managed.

'What will you have, Ella?' his Mom asked me.

I couldn't see Aarav. Maybe he had gone inside to change.

'Nothing, Aunty.' I said. 'We just had snacks.'

'So what? You are young boys and girls. You should eat a lot. You need lots of protein.'

I smiled. 'Aunty, why do you take so much pain. You are not well.' I said, holding her hands.

'I never enter the kitchen. He does everything.' She pointed towards her son, who was back by then, changing in casuals. He was looking handsome, even in casuals.

'He cooks?'

'Yes. He cooks and washes dishes as well. He can do everything. He washes my clothes before going to the office.'

'That's impressive.'

'I have no one except for him.' She said. 'He had appointed a maid for me. She left stealing money and utensils.'

Aarav giggled at this.

'Beta, make something for Ella. She has come for the first time.' She instructed her son.

I protested again but in vain. Nobody listened to me. I saw a few English novels on the wooden table. I asked aunty about them.

She said, 'we both read a lot. We have no one in Kolkata. After his father's death, we didn't even get any help from the government immediately. We had to leave the quarter, so I decided to come here, in Kolkata. This is my parents' flat. They died long ago. As I am their only child, I got this flat luckily.'

'What about pension money?' I asked.

'Yeah, I receive a pension.' She said. 'It takes a little time. Everything doesn't happen immediately, dear.' She smiled at the end of the sentence.

We talked about different English classics. She told me that she doesn't like to watch daily soaps on TV. She only watches TV for news and sports. She showed me her room that had many books piled up at a corner table. I saw her husband's photo on her bedroom wall. His face matched Aarav a lot. He got his father's complexion and face and his mother's physique.

'He died of a heart attack in the field. Can you imagine?' aunty said. 'He was always a very fit army man.'

I kept quiet.

'After his death, I also got heart problems.'

'You will be fine, aunty.' I assured her.

We came back to the sofa. Aarav had made bread *pakoras* and tea. He was pretty fast in cooking. I took one *pakora* and drank tea with aunty. The bread *pakora* tasted nice. He was a good cook for sure.

Aarav's world was so different from mine. His world was sober. Mine was chaotic. He was pretty organised. On the other hand, I was a mess.

xii

'Ella.' Dad's voice woke me up from a sweet dream. I don't precisely remember the dream. But I was there sitting at a coffee table with a cup of smoking hot tea and a cup of coffee. And yes, I remember, Aarav was there!

'Yes, Dad.' I yawned. 'What are you doing in my room?'

'Your Mom's away. I'm cooking. What will you eat at breakfast?'

'Where's Mom?'

'She has gone to meet her friend, Janki.'

'What happened to Janki aunty now?'

'She has fallen off the staircase. Now she needs help.'

'Poor Janki aunty!' I turned to the other side. 'She's so alone in the world. Why doesn't she marry again?' I yawned again. 'She should adopt a kid.'

'Marrying again can be a great option for her. But she doesn't want that. It's her life, let her make her own choice.' Dad said, smiling. 'Everyone is not blessed with a family, dear.' He paused and put a hand on my head. 'Tell me what will you have?'

'Anything will do.' I was still on the bed.

'Get up, Ella.' He said. 'It's already 8:15.'

'15 minutes more, Dad.' I was still sleepy. I covered my face with a pillow.

'Kailash is there for a few more days, Ella. You have to learn to tackle his work until somebody new is appointed.' He said.

Well, sleep disappeared. I was wide awake now. I had thirteen more days to investigate and bring out the truth. I dialed my Watson when Dad left my room.

'Hello, Ma'am. Good Morning.' He instantly picked my call. He was panting.

'Good Morning. You are so fast at picking calls nowadays.' I said. 'Why are you panting, by the way?'

'I understand the importance of some particular calls.' He quickly said. 'And I just returned from jogging.'

Impressive! With a brain exercise, the man also cares for body exercises.

I smiled. 'No yoga today?'

'Don't get time every day.' He said.

'Can you come half an hour earlier?' I asked, changing the topic.

'Yeah, sure.' He said.

'Thanks.'

'Did Sherlock ever thank Watson for doing his duty?'

I laughed.

'Don't forget that they are friends.' He added.

'Yea... I will not forget. We are friends now.'

'Yes, Sherlock.' He said.

I had worn a new pair of jeans and shirt that day with matching earrings and pendant. Also, I matched my shoes with my shirt and lipstick. I unbuttoned two top buttons of my shirt through which the pendent dazzled.

'You are looking great.' Was the first thing that Aarav told me entering the cabin. I had reached before him. He was wearing a white shirt that fit his body perfectly. It was tailor-made for sure. And I should have thanked the tailor.

'Thanks.' I said, smiling quickly. In the office, I am professional. However, it was always very tough to act professionally with Aarav.

'Ma'am, so what are we going to do?' he asked, sitting across me.

'Aarav, did Kailash ever tell you anything about his financial problems?'

'No. He doesn't speak much with me. He hates me,' he said, 'Actually, he never likes my company. Not even when we were in school.'

'Why?'

'That's weird. He thinks I am smarter than him.' He chuckled at the end. 'In fact, he thinks that everyone is smarter than him.'

'He's a total weirdo.'

'Totally.' He chuckled again.

'Who is the real culprit?'

'Don't know, Ma'am. But I think we should keep an eye on Nehal as well.'

'Why?' I asked.

'I saw Nehal talking to a person standing at the main gate of the office. Seeing me, the man disappeared. Nehal lied to me saying that he was not talking to anyone. If it's not fishy, then why did he hide? Plus, his desktop is the only one on the floor with password protection.'

'Why didn't you tell me about this earlier?'

'You were new then. I never thought that it's important to tell you. But I think it has something to do with Kailash's resignation.' He said.

'Well, Aarav, come quick. We have to check Nehal's computer.'

'What? We will spy on his computer?'

'Yes. We have rights as detectives.'

'That's...'

'What?'

'Okay.'

'C'mon.'

We rushed to Nehal's computer. As I powered it on, the Windows screen started.

I sat on the chair. Aarav stood behind me with a tensed look on his face. Once he was too close that I felt his warm breath on my shoulder. Well, I managed to stay professional.

'It's asking for a password. You are right. It's password protected.' I said.

Aarav's forehead got more curves. 'Try MUSE.' He said.

'Okay.' I typed in "MUSE" like an obedient person. But it didn't open. I looked at him.

'Try Nehal Singh.'

It didn't work this time as well.

'Get up.' Aarav ordered me.

'Excuse me. Are we quitting?'

'No. We are playing smarter.'

'For that, I have to get up?' I said while leaving the chair to him.

He sat down and guarded the keyboard from me.

'What are you typing?'

The windows opened.

'Wow, you cracked it! What did you type?'

'You don't need to know.' He grinned sheepishly.

'Tell me. It's my order.'

'BigBoobs.'

'Huh?' My eyes automatically went to my boobs.

'No. I mean the password is "BigBoobs".' He looked away.

'*Tharki...*' I addressed it to Nehal. But he thought that it was for him. He looked at me with protest.

'It's Nehal's favorite phrase.' He laughed loudly.

'Seriously?' I said, 'and how do you know that?'

'Boys talk, you know.'

We both shared a burst of mild laughter without looking at each other.

Things were getting more comfortable and friendlier between Aarav and me. On the other side of the ocean, the waves broke apart from each other. They were beating hard on my heart. I was afraid to discover what was in Nehal's computer. I secretly prayed for nothing wrong to come out.

Aarav went through all the folders one by one. We couldn't gather anything fishy. Everything was extra clean on his computer.

'There must be some hidden file.' I suggested.

'It's a new desktop, remember? The old one is tampered by someone.'

'I don't suffer from memory loss, Aarav. The old hard drive is totally damaged, I know.' I said. 'I am searching for recent files.'

'You are behaving like Sherlock.' He giggled.

'I am sure, Aarav, there must be something if he's the culprit.'

'You wanna check?' he asked me.

'Yeah.' I sat in front of the computer, and the next thing which I did is a real crime.

It took three minutes to get into the hidden files of Nehal's computer. All Hail to the Ethical Hacking courses I have done in college and practiced it various times to hack my friend's computers.

'Are you hacking?' Aarav went closer to the computer screen.

'Yes.' I said. 'Shut your mouth, please!'

'Hacking is a crime.' He managed to mumble.

'It's called ethical hacking.' I said.

I liked the shocked expression on his face. His face lightened up when I found a hidden folder in Nehal's computer.

'What's that?' I asked.

'I have no idea.' He mumbled gently. My heart started beating faster. I hoped that his heart too started hammering in the same way.

I opened the folder. There was an Excel sheet, named "Customer_Data".

My hand shook while I clicked on the file. A long Excel sheet opened. There were four columns, namely, "Date", "Customers", "Seller", and "Cost".

'What the fuck is this?' I shouted.

Aarav didn't utter a word. He almost snatched the mouse from me. He started scrolling down.

'These customers are not our customers. And who's the seller? Farya? Who's that?' he said after sometimes.

'Farya?' I went the closest I could to the screen. 'Farya Malik! What the fuck!!!' I left the chair.

'Do you know her?' Aarav asked me. At that moment, I felt like shouting on him for not knowing his boss'- temporary boss'- real name.

'Farya Malik is my name.' I shouted. 'All the transactions have been done by my name!'

'What?' He was astonished. His eyes were wide opened. 'This is fucking crazy!'

'Yes!'

'Now if you expose this sheet you will be labeled as a cheater, a smuggler and a...'

'Shut up, Aarav!' I said, 'Will you stop labeling me a criminal?'

'Wait for a moment, Ella.' He took my name. He forgot to call me ma'am. 'Let's imagine the situation' he continued, 'the products started missing from the company, you join MUSE, Kailash threatens you to leave MUSE, Nehal's computer gets tampered, somebody abused you through a message on the computer, his computer was changed, Kailash accepts that he is guilty of the smuggles, he resigns after that without giving a proper reason, Nehal's computer has a hidden folder with a transaction sheet with your name as the seller of the products. And I am pretty sure that the customers are from the black market.' He paused. He looked at me in a worried look, 'Do you understand the chronology?'

'I am in a great mess!'

'Indeed, you are!' he whispered.

'Aarav, copy this file and give it to me in a pen drive. I want to check Kailash's computer as well. But it's too late now. They will arrive at any time.'

'Yeah...'

We already had lost every bit of energy at that time. We decided not to ask Nehal anything about the file that day and secretly keep an eye on him. It was a devastating feeling. If the file ever comes out, I would be accused of stealing my company's products and selling in the black market.

God, where I was trapped!

I switched off the AC of my cabin and opened the door. From my chair, I could see everyone coming in. Kailash came first. His eyes met mine as he greeted me. I nodded coldly. I found it difficult to nod even. I was lost in thoughts.

Ali entered after him and did not even notice my door opened. Nehal came after a minute or two and greeted louder. Amar came after him and gave a surprising look at the opened gate. He peeped in the cabin. Seeing me, he apologized for peeping and greeted me. I saw Amod getting a cup of coffee for someone.

Nobody ordered him. That clears out the fact that somebody drinks coffee just after entering the office and Amod knew it.

'I suggest you close the door.' Aarav said from his workplace.

I kept quiet. He got up from his place and walked towards the door. He went outside, closing the door behind him.

I took my phone in my hand. It had one WhatsApp message from Mom. She had written, "Have lunch on time".

I read it and closed the WhatsApp window. I went to the contact list. I typed "d" in the search bar of the contact list. The first contact that starts with "d" was the person I wanted to call.

'Hello, Ella?' The surprised voice rang up on the other side of the phone.

'Hi, *Dadi*.' I said in a sober tone. 'How are you?'

'I am fine, beta. How are you? How are you doing in MUSE?'

'I am not okay, *Dadi*.' I broke down crying.

'What happened to my little girl?' *Dadi's* voice became worried. 'What's bothering you, dear?'

'*Dadi*, things are going against me in MUSE.' I wept on. 'I don't deserve MUSE.'

'Who told you that you don't deserve MUSE?'

'I know, *Dadi*. It's not my thing. I don't belong here. The people do not like me here. I can't let Dad know about their hatred towards me.'

'Ella, I admit that you are very new to all these. There was a time when your Dad was also new to all these. He managed it, right? See, where he is now…'

I wept again.

'Beta, my little munchkin, please, don't cry.' She said. 'Everything gets better with time. It's your time now to fight with equal intensity for what you have. Don't give up, Ella. You are my strongest *baccha*.'

'*Dadi*, do you think I can stand in this men-dominated business environment?'

'Why not? Gender doesn't matter in business, Ella. It's your brain that works there. Keep your brain clean and work hard. Don't forget that you are your father's daughter, Ella. You are my son's daughter. And your *Dadi* knows everything but defeat. Your *Dadi* doesn't like defeated people.'

'*Dadi*, somebody abused me a few days back. He said that I was undeserving.'

'Maybe you are, currently undeserving. Remember one thing, Ella, you are a daughter now. Your father needs you right now. And I know that you are capable of turning yourself to a deserving boss from a responsible daughter.' She paused. I also kept quiet.

'It's your test, Ella. You have to fight on your own. You have to complete the journey on your own. And your *Dadi* trusts you.'

Aarav was back with two cups of coffee. He placed one on my table without uttering a single word and turned on the AC. He went to his place with his cup.

I wiped my tears. I hang up the phone. *Dadi* asked me to focus on work. I didn't complain about not having tea but coffee. I took my cup of coffee and sipped it with teary eyes and a running nose.

xiii

In the evening, Sudhir called in my cabin.

'Ma'am, a supplier is seriously troubling us. Please do something.'

I checked the clock.

'Sudhir, it's time to leave.' I said. 'How can I meet someone now?'

'Ma'am, he is saying that if we do not order in bulk, he will not supply from now onwards.'

Good Heaven!

'Let me talk to Dad and get back to you tomorrow.' I said to Sudhir.

'Okay, Ma'am. I'm asking him to come tomorrow.'

'He can call, right? He doesn't need to come.'

'Okay, Ma'am.' Sudhir hung up.

I dialed another number on my phone.

'Haris, can I come to your flat for a stay?'

'Sure.' He chuckled. 'You were scheduled to come today. It's all yours.'

'I am not kidding.' I was frustrated, broken from inside, and tired. I didn't want to face Dad in this tough situation. I had to talk about supplier issues, though.

'What happened, Ella?' He sensed the situation.

'What's wrong?'

'Everything is wrong here, Haris.' I couldn't help it. I cried, sitting in the office only. Luckily the door was closed, and Aarav was not there.

'Ella...' Haris was confused. His voice said so. 'I am coming to your office to pick you up. We can talk about the problem; whatever it is, okay?'

'Hmm.' I disconnected the call and broke down crying.

For the first time in my life, I genuinely wanted to help Dad. I left my job and hang up my MBA plan to care for MUSE, to lift MUSE from its distress, and most importantly, to lower down Dad's burden. Why God doesn't let me do good things? What's wrong with me?

'Ma'am?' a shocked voice hit my brain. With teary eyes, I lifted my head. I could figure him out with teary veils over my eyes. He must have never been that much shocked in his entire life. I forgot to wipe my tears away. I cried more, seeing him. I was seated in my chair. I lowered my face and held it between my palms, crying louder this time.

'What's there to cry like this?' his unprepared voice interrupted my cry.

'I don't know what to do, Aarav. It's not what I expected... why me?'

He closed the door and locked it from inside. He stepped towards me slowly and stood by my side. The next thing that happened soothed me but put me in shock like hell.

He grabbed me by my shoulder and pulled me closer. As I was sitting and he was standing beside me, my head touched his belly. So, that's how our first hug happened most unexpectedly and awkwardly.

'Did you ask the same question when you had come to know that you are one of the chosen ones for this company's future?' He mumbled. 'Things are not worst. You are clean and innocent. MUSE belongs to you, Ella. You are a game-changer. And you have to change the game when it's time.'

I wiped my tears. His hands were still on my shoulder. My heart rate was higher than usual, not only with his touch and his strong perfume but also by his words. It was magical. It was soothing and was healing me from inside, forcing me to lift my soul. As soon as I freed myself from him, he handed me a tissue box and a water bottle. I took a large sip while wiping my face and eyes with the tissue. Aarav stood straight beside me.

'Ella, we can sort it out. Don't worry.' He said, breaking the silence.

'The transaction is being done for a year, Aarav. Why didn't Dad notice it ever?' I asked slowly.

'We badly need CCTVs in the office.' he said after sometimes.

'That can't happen, you already know.'

He nodded.

'We can't offend Dad and his ideologies, but we have to find out the culprit.'

'Do you think it's Nehal?' Aarav asked.

'He's not absolutely out of it. After all, the files are found on his computer only. If he knows about the file and he is the culprit, how does he keep himself so calm as if he's innocent?'

'Maybe because he's actually innocent.' He said. I kept quiet. He threw another question at me. 'What about Kailash? He said that he smuggled them.'

'He's lying.' I was very sure of it, so I said the words loudly.

'I think we should talk to Nehal and ask everything out.'

'That may make him aware of the fact that we know everything.'

'That's right.'

'My head is spinning. I am not going home tonight. I'll be at Haris' place tonight. Make sure Dad doesn't come to know about any of this.'

He nodded.

'By the way, will you talk to Dad about the supplier issue that happened today?'

'Sure. I will. You can relax.'

I smiled at him, plainly. He reverted.

'Open the door.' I pointed towards the door.

'Oh...sorry.' He actually had forgotten about it, I guess. He rushed towards it and opened it.

Haris called at 7 to inform me that he would be a little late in arriving at my place. So, I stayed in the office alone. Aarav assured before leaving that he would do his best to make things right all over again in MUSE and I should relax.

I informed Mom about not coming home. She didn't ask many questions.

I waited alone for Haris in the office. I sat on the couch, blankly.

You know what? To me, the family business felt like period cramps. They give you immense pain until they bleed it out. But when they don't happen at the right time, you get worried about them. You have an emotional and tragic attachment to them. Without caring for them, you just can't do.

I was attached to MUSE in every way just like I am connected to my period cramps.

When I told this to Kaira, she said that it was the worst comparison she has ever come across. Whatever!

I was, by now, emotionally and tragically attached to MUSE. I couldn't give up now.

When period cramps trouble you, visit a doctor. Don't cut off your ovaries, C'mon!

'Ma'am, your friend is here to pick you up.' The watchman informed me.

I took my bag and walked out of the cabin. I climbed down the stairs slowly and came out on the road.

'Get in, quick.' Haris popped his head out of the car window. 'The traffic police are so adamant here.'

'What happened?' I asked, getting in.

'They just can't let me park anywhere.' He was upset.

'That happens. This is Kolkata.'

'Areyy... how will you know what happens? You don't drive. Your cars are resting under your building, and you are traveling in an auto or a cab. Hail Ola and Uber! Seriously annoying.'

'I don't know driving, you know that.' I said.

'And I told you a thousand times to learn driving.' He said.

'Yeah... but...'

'You always give an excuse. Now you are at MUSE. You are the boss. Learn driving for God's sake. Who knows when you need your driving skill?'

'You are right.' I accepted my fault without extending the conversation.

'What if you have to chase the culprit who is running away in a Bolero? Call Ola to follow him?' he said. This was seriously lame. I didn't laugh. He laughed on his own joke and turned silent understanding the inappropriateness of his joke. He focused on the road.

For a moment, I sat quietly in the passenger seat and Haris drove silently. Once we left Science City Crossing, the road was quite emptier.

'What happened to you? Did you cry?' Haris broke the silence.

'The unexpected happened, Haris.' I said.

'You are sweating even in the A.C.' he said.

I smirked, turning outside.

'Okay, you can tell me when you feel like it. Till then, let me speak. I have something to tell you.'

I turned to him, 'What?'

'I broke up with Manisha, finally.' He said. I had forgotten about her existence even.

'Yeah, so? Isn't that very much predictable?'

'I thought for this time a girl would actually like to stick to me.' He laughed. 'But, no. When she heard that I have applied for a transfer in the US, she gave a red signal.'

'You know what's wrong with you, Haris?' I leaned towards him. 'You try to find love after making love. You should first find love then make love.'

'Ahhh.... my best friend really grew up. Talking mature, huh?' He laughed.

'Do you think I'm kidding?' I felt serious.

'Oh...no no.' He laughed again. 'You have a valid point.' He said. 'Finding love... making love... first making love...'

'...first finding love.' I corrected him. This time I also laughed with him. 'Then making love.'

'Then, she will stay?'

'I think so.' I said.

'Isn't that what you exactly tried to do with Resham?' he said, gently but sarcastically.

I fell silent for a moment. 'Yes. I did try to do that only. And I failed.'

'Means there's no guarantee in your theory.'

'First of all, it's not a theory. It's quite practical. Second of all, Resham was a scoundrel. I should thank God a hundred times for my break up with Resham. Because if I didn't break up with him, I would have never fallen for Aarav.'

'WHAT?' he made the car to a halt. 'What did you just say? Do you love Aarav? When did it all happen?'

'Drive, please.' I raised a brow at him.

'No, tell me first.'

'Drive, Haris! People are honking behind.' I shouted at him. He drove the car. But he didn't stop talking for a moment.

'I think I am in love with him.' I shouted to shut him up. 'I THINK!'

'Oh well...' he chuckled. 'You are so selfish. You didn't tell me that you love him.'

'I said "I think".' I made quotations with my fingers in the air to emphasize "I think".

'Why do you think so?'

'Because I can feel what he wants to say. He can snatch words from my mouth. We understand each other so much. He supports me in everything, you know. He does everything that Resham didn't do.'

Haris didn't reply. He was quiet as well. Soon we reached his apartment. I got out of the car. He threw the apartment keys to me.

'I thought that my best friend would freak out hearing that I have decided to move out of the country.' He said, popping his head out of the window. 'But she did not even react a bit.'

I smiled at him. 'I heard you already, Haris. Come upstairs.'

I proceeded towards the building while he went to park the car. Haris always had a dream of going out of the country. It significantly grew stronger after his parent's death.

Just when I reached the lift and pressed the switch, my phone rang up. It was in my bag. I grabbed it lazily thinking it to be Haris kidding around, but my face became pale once I saw the screen.

It flashed with "Dad".

'Hello.' I picked the call and said. In the next second, I cleared my throat. It was jamming with each passing second.

'Where are you?' His hoarse voice spoke up on the other side.

'Dad,' I felt my throat jamming again, 'I am at a friend's place.'

'Why? You should be home, right?'

Should I?

'Yes, Dad.' I gently spoke up.

'Then why are you not home? You should act more responsible now, you know that, right? Don't I need to talk to you regarding work? Don't you want to report to me about today's job?'

Dad threw questions after questions. He wasn't angry. But he was disappointed. My eyes filled with tears. Why do I make such mistakes?

'Dad, I'm coming home soon.' I managed to speak up.

'Not needed.' He said firmly. I already took the report from Aarav. He mailed me everything and told me about the supplier issue.'

'I'm sorry, Dad. I should have...'

'Listen, Ella.' Dad's voice was firm as usual. 'I expect to get reports from you not Aarav.' He paused.

'Yes, Dad. Okay.'

'And we are not ordering in bulk. The company is still suffering financially. If the supplier wants to stop supplying, he can do so. We can't do anything about that.'

'Okay. Dad, I can come home now.'

'No, Ella. Stay there. See you tomorrow. And please have dinner properly.' He said and disconnected the call.

With an irritating and heartbreaking beep, Dad was off from the phone. The lift already opened and closed in the meantime. I had to press the button again.

Haris arrived.

'Why are you still standing here?' he asked, looking shocked. 'Oh wait, are you crying again?' he was puzzled now.

'No...'

He stared at my face.

'Yes.' I wept louder.

xiv

'What the fuck are you saying?' Haris almost tripped over the doormat after hearing about the secret files in Nehal's computer. I told him in the lift.

'Somebody wants to screw me up in the worst possible way.' I threw myself on the sofa in his drawing-room. He landed beside me.

'But why?'

'I don't know. I am crying for the whole day.'

'That's stupid.' He commented. 'You should find out the culprit. I think it is Nehal only. He is doing everything and blackmailing Kailash to take all the blame on his shoulder.'

'Blackmailing for what?'

'It can be anything. Kailash must have done something in life that Nehal knows.'

'You are reading Agatha Christie.' I said, frustrated.

'No...' he protested. 'That's what I think. Really.' I kept quiet. He really had a point.

'Do one thing, for some days, try to keep an eye on Kailash and Nehal.' He suggested.

I nodded in affirmation. 'I can't keep an eye on them. But Aarav can.'

'Then make him work. After all, he knows everyone better than you do.'

I nodded again.

'Okay, now I'm hungry. I have to freshen up and cook.' He said.

'Why don't you get a maid for yourself?' I said, laying on the sofa.

'I don't like anyone's cooking but for me. Thanks for the suggestion and go get freshen up, please. I am making *cutting chai* for you.'

The *'cutting chai'* part energized me of all the things he said. There was a smile on my face. I got up quickly from the sofa.

'Can I borrow your T-shirt?'

'I hate this part the most.'

I laughed and quickly gave him a peck on his cheek.

'I hate you.' He managed to say in between.

I laughed again. I gave him a quick hug and went to his room to grab a T-shirt. I finally found a yellow T-shirt that I had gifted him on his last birthday. I grabbed it, smiling. Haris always keeps my gifts safely. Even if the T-shirt is torn, he will keep it. He never throws away anything given by me. Haris and I share a special bond. We fought a thousand times, but again we are always there for each other. I knew he would cheer me up. Though Dad was offended for not returning home tonight this night stay will help for sure.

My parents want me to get married to Haris because maybe they understand OUR understanding better than us. This is quite confusing, and I will never marry Haris, but it's proof of our bonding. Haris became successful in life before anyone in our batch. He was not a very bright student, but he was always smart and talented. I always knew that he would work hard and stand on his feet soon. However, sleeping with his previous boss and Manisha wasn't a smart option.

My mother is always so pleased with him. Dad plays chess with him for hours on weekends. And in their mind, they frame him as my groom every day.

However, the scene is different on our end. Haris has only one dream – to settle in the US. He has no plan of getting married before 35. On the other hand, I never felt any sort of 'marriage' thing with Haris. We are too different from each other.

Well, now people would say, opposite attracts and make a family. That's right. For that, you can pick your own choice of vehicle and cross the same road together. In our case, our vehicles and our roads both are different. So, we never got along and settle down for marriage. Though we never declared anything officially.

I went to the bathroom and took a bath. I felt relaxed. I changed into his T-shirt and came out only to find him sitting on the sofa with a teapot.

'Oh already done?'

'Yes, it doesn't take an eternity to make tea.' He mocked. I giggled.

'Are you sure about Aarav?' he suddenly asked.

I looked at him sharply. He was sitting on the sofa, and I was standing right in front of him. He grabbed my hand and made me sit beside him.

'Ella, are you seriously in love with Aarav?' he asked again.

I kept quiet for some moment. What the heck with him? Why was he so much into my feelings for Aarav?

'I am falling for him gradually.' I said, getting a burning sensation on my cheeks. I couldn't contact my eyes with him.

'That's great.' He said. He left the sofa instantly and went inside. I was puzzled. I looked at his way for sometimes clueless.

I served myself tea, not getting anything to do. He came back in casuals - black track pants and a white T-Shirt. I smiled at him holding his cup of tea.

'Thanks.' He said, sitting beside me. He didn't counter smile, though.

'What happened?' I asked, putting my left leg on the right.

'You look sexy like this.' He said, smiling.

'Yeah. I know.' I giggled. 'Is that the reason for your seriousness?'

'No.' He smiled again. 'Aarav is lucky.'

'Oh, wait.' I put my cup down on the table. 'Are you jealous?'

'No.' He looked at me. 'I am protective of my best friend. I don't want him to be Resham at any chance.'

'He won't.' I said. 'He's very different.'
'What if he is behind all of this and trying to help you to impress you?'

'Huh?' I sat straight.

'Just think like this, Ella.' He curled his legs up on the sofa and turned to me. He made me face him. We sat on the sofa, curling our legs up and facing each other. He continued, 'Aarav has the intention of overtaking your Dad's business. He tries to create a problem. You join MUSE, and he gets the chance. He behaves nicely with you. You discuss the problems openly with him. And then, he helps you in every way. That way, he has profit and profit... and lots of profit... and finally...'

'Stop.' I had to cut him.

He took a deep breath.

'I can't buy this.' I said. 'He can't do all these.'

'Why can't you buy this?' he asked, looking straight into my eyes.

'Because he doesn't release that vibe.'

'Okay.' He smiled and turned away. He finished his tea. Took out a packet of biscuits from under the table and tore the packet with force. Few biscuits jumped out and fell everywhere. Some fell on me as well. One half-broken biscuit landed on my bare thigh. He picked it up and brushed the powdered pieces away from my thighs with his fingers and put it in his mouth.

'Haris, you have a valid point.' I broke the ice.

'I know.' He said, eating biscuits.

'But I still can't buy it. Aarav is not a guy like that. You should meet him.'

'Biscuits?'

'No.'

'Cigarette?'

'Do you have a "Navy Cut"?'

'Yes.' He replied after thinking for sometimes.

'But why do you want that particular brand?' he giggled.

'That was the brand we smoked for the first time together in college, remember?'

'Oh yes...' he got the energy. 'I remember. In Pinto's *pan* shop.'

'Yeah. You coughed. I didn't.'

'I was almost choking on it.' he laughed. 'Do you remember, that geek of our class, what was his name...' he scratched his head, 'Ayan.'

'...had said that we have to go through a cancer test soon.' I completed it for him.

'Yes. Oh, my God! He was such a dumbass.' We fell on the floor laughing our lungs out.

'Wait, let me bring it.' he got up the floor. I laid there, staring at the ceiling and laughing.

He came back after two minutes with a lighted Navy Cut between his fingers. I took it from him between my fingers.

'On a serious note, smoking kills.' He said.

'Thanks for the disclaimer.' I said, taking a big puff.

'You should leave this habit, Ella.'

'Hmm...'

'I am serious about this.' He said, laying beside me. Both of us put our legs up on the sofa and laid on the cold floor.

'I am not a regular smoker, you know that.'

'Did you see anywhere written "regular smoking kills"?' he questioned.

'Haha.'

'Does Aarav smoke?' He asked.

'I don't think anyone in the office smoke.' I said.

'Shame on you.' He laughed. I laughed with him too. But it was a short one. Then we stayed silent for some time.

'Haris, why didn't you ever think of dating me? We are friends since ninth standard and us, I think, we know each other the most.'

'That's why I'll never date you.' He chuckled. 'I know you are better at giving relationship advice than me, but there is one advice that I wanna give you.'

'Tell me.' I said, throwing the burnt cigarette away from the window behind the sofa. We could see a black veil of night from that window.

'Never date a person if you know him or her totally.' I laughed out loud. But he didn't join me.

He continued, 'It is never a good decision to date the person you know the best. You should leave that relationship to friendship only. That keeps the relationship healthy.'

'Who taught you all these?' I was amazed. 'Manisha?' I laughed. This time, he too.

'I am not that naive.' He added. 'I hope your parents understand that as well and stop looking at me every time like they are looking at their son-in-law.'

I laughed again. 'This is hilarious. I have to inform them that you are leaving India soon. They will be so sad.' I made a sad face. But it made him laugh as the face was funny.

'I think you should tell them about Aarav instead.' He said. 'At least they will shift the focus to him.' He giggled. 'I just hope he's the good guy.'

'Come here.' I grabbed him close. 'Don't worry about Aarav. I am shattered while saying this, but we have no future together. Plus I am not sure if he has the same feelings for me. Better not talk or think about this.'

'C'mon.' He hugged me. 'His actions say that he is attached to you emotionally.'

'What if he isn't attached emotionally?'

'Then he's the culprit and my theory about him is right.'

'That's rude.'

He laughed. I also joined him. We laughed wholeheartedly.

The next day I went to office from Haris' place wearing unwashed clothes. Okay, I used his perfumes to cover the bad smell of my sweaty clothes from the last day. Aarav smiled at me as soon as I entered the cabin.

'Hi.' I counter smiled, greeting him.

'Hello. How are you today?'

'Holding up together.'

He smiled.

'May I come in?' The voice came from behind. I turned back.

'Oh, Ali. Come in.' I said.

'Good morning.' He said, getting in the cabin.

'Good morning.' I said. 'You want to say anything?'

'I just wanted to know if everything is all right?'

I stood as I was. Ali was facing me. Aarav was at his place standing by the table. I was thinking about what to answer to this unexpected question from an unexpected person at an unexpected time. I was pretty sure that Aarav's mind was grooving in the same line.

'Yeah. Everything is... okay.' I said.

'I mean, did you come to know who tampered Nehal's computer and wrote those... you know...' he looked down.

'No. I don't know. I think it was a bad prank. I should ignore it.' I moved towards my seat.

'Oh...' he hesitated a bit. 'And about the lost properties?'

'No.' I said. 'I think we should deploy CCTVs in the office.'

'That's great.' He said. 'Okay.' He turned back. 'I should go... loads of work left...' he went out mumbling.

I had intentionally lied about the CCTV. If there was a culprit in the office he would be aware now by this piece of the news.

'I have some news for you.' Aarav said as soon as Ali left the room. I looked at him. 'I followed Nehal yesterday. He met a man in the adjacent lane. When he came out, he had two laptop bags with him.'

'For how long he was with the man?'

'Almost five minutes.'

'Why did you follow?'

'Because I am Watson.'

I smiled plainly. His joke didn't turn my mood on. He understood that.

'Ella, I have doubt on him from the very beginning. I think he is behind all of these. Not Kailash.'

'Hmm.'

I fell silent. I didn't get words to speak.

'Ella. There's one more thing...'

'Say.'

'Today's is Amar's birthday.'

'Let's celebrate.'

Well, the birthday celebration was not a part of MUSE. Amar was the first guy whose birthday was celebrated in MUSE. That too, with a three-layered cake and twenty-one candles. Oh well, He was given a Sonata watch as a gift as well.

'What should I write in accounts for this birthday celebration?' Aarav asked me after the so-called party.

'Olive oil for Employees.' I answered, sitting on my seat.

'Huh?' and the next second, he burst out laughing. He got the sarcasm. I smiled.

xv

'Ella, try to spend the night at your own house at least on the weekdays.' Dad's heavy voice rang up as soon as I stepped into the house.

'Sure, Dad.' I said, proceeding towards my room.

'Wait up.' Dad interrupted me.

I stopped and walked towards him. He was checking some files sitting in the drawing-room. I stood in front of the table. He lifted his face and stared at my face sometimes. I looked away.

'What about the office? Are they reporting to you regularly?'

'Yes, Dad. Except for Ali, everyone reports to me every day after work.'

'That's great.' He said. He opened a red file. It was Ali's file. 'His work has the lowest success rate.'

'Why?' I said. 'He's the senior engineer. I put the heavy works on his account only. I gave him almost sixty-two motherboards and twelve laptops to repair last week.'

'Twelve laptops?' he looked at me, surprised. 'But he only reported ten to me.' He pointed to the file.'

I leaned on the table to take a closer look at it. Ten laptops were reported among which five are repaired, and five are marked as 'non-repairable'.

'I remember clearly, Dad. I gave him twelve.'

'Then where's the other two?' Dad's face looked pale. His forehead got unusual lines. My stomach started cramping with a predictable fear.

'Is it possible that he forgot to report about those two?'

'No.' Dad stressed out. He was up from his chair. 'I even had asked him why there are only five fixed out of ten? He said that the success rate is 50% now. He is trying to increase it.' Dad said. 'He didn't even mention that it was twelve, not ten.'

'Where are the laptops, Dad?' My face started sweating. 'Is it possible that they are in the office somewhere or misplaced in someone's desk?'

'It never happened.' Dad became restless. He almost fell on the sofa. Mom came out in the drawing-room. Kaira also joined shortly.

'Dad, things started to go missing for a year, right?' I asked, sitting beside Dad. I handed him a water bottle. 'Before that, it never happened.'

'How do you know that they are going missing for a year?'

'I have proof, Dad. Maybe you didn't notice it before two RAMs went missing.' I said, 'No, it's time to catch the culprit, Dad. Aarav saw Nehal meeting with random strangers outside the office many times. He told me. He also saw Nehal yesterday talking to someone, and he had two laptop bags with him.'

'Nehal?'

'Yes, Dad. Nehal. He can smuggle things from the office. He can do it right under our nose.'

'But Nehal is a good guy. He...'

'Dad, stop trusting people blindly.'

I said this little louder. Dad was cut short. He drank some water.

'But what's the proof that Nehal had those two laptops? It can be his personal belongings as well.'

'Do you have proof that it was his personal belongings?'

'No...'

'Dad, we should charge him. He has all the facilities for smuggling things from Ali's desk and selling it in the black market. Those strangers are his customers.' I made my point.

Dad was quite broken. He stopped talking. Mom sat on the other side of him.

'Ella is right. This can happen.' Mom said. 'You can't trust anyone blindly.'

'I pay them quite well, Salma.' Dad softly said to Mom. 'Why will they do such things?'

'You only say, Dad, that this is a king's business. People become millionaires overnight. Those laptops cost almost forty to fifty thousand each. Do you understand the revenue, Dad?'

Everyone was silent for sometimes.

'Dad,' I put my hand on his hands, 'don't worry. I will find the culprit out and put an end to this. Trust me, please!'

'What will you do? I don't understand anything...'

'Dad, please, for once, trust me the way you trust your employees.' I got tears in my eyes, 'Please!'

He nodded. He put his hand on my head for a brief second and felt absolutely silent. Mom and Kaira left him alone. I went to freshen up.

When I came out of the washroom, Mom was in my room with a glass of Glucon-D. Her face had clear signs of worry.

I took the glass from her. 'Thanks, Mom, I need this.'

'What are you hiding from your Dad, Ella?' she asked.

The glass had just touched my lips. Even before sipping it, I had to stop. Mom's question hit my stomach hard. I put the glass down.

'I am not hiding anything.' I said, looking away.

'You can't make eye-contact. You are lying, Ella.' She said.

'Mom, Dad won't be able to take it.' I turned to her. 'The matter is crucial. And worst. And unexpected and...'

'Tell me the truth.' She commanded.

'Mom...'

'Tell me, Ella.' She was louder now. 'If you think that hiding it from your Dad will help him, then you are wrong. He should know everything. MUSE is his. Not yours, Ella. You have no authority to hide information.'

'Come out.' I told her and went outside. 'Where's Dad gone?'

'He's in the terrace, I guess.' Kaira said.

'Mom, I'll tell everything to Dad. After that, if he gets a heart attack, you will be responsible.'

'What are you saying?' Mom shouted at me following me.

I broke stairs in hare's speed to reach the terrace.

'Dad.' I called for him from the stairs only. I reached the terrace panting. Dad was surprised to see me on the terrace panting and calling him like a mad girl. He was more surprised seeing Mom there because Mom never climbed the terrace for a year due to her arthritis pain.

'What happened?' he was sitting on a plastic chair in our terrace garden. He got up from it.

'Dad, I didn't tell you the complete truth. I hide many things from you from the very beginning.' I started. Mom stood behind me with a worried and angry face. The expression was very peculiar to see on her face.

I continued, 'The day I called for the meeting in office after joining MUSE, you remember Dad?' he nodded in affirmation, I said, 'I didn't just give them the task of introducing themselves. I talked about the lost RAMs.' Dad stared at my face without any expression. I went on, 'Even then I didn't know that our properties are getting smuggled in the black market. I thought that it was lost or replaced due to someone's irresponsibility. I developed a quest to find out the truth. A day after that, Nehal's computer was found tampered. Somebody had done it before the office hour or maybe after the office hour the previous day.' I stopped.

'Tampered?' Dad was shocked.

'Yes. Not only tampered. Somebody had used his monitor as a writing pad and abused me scratching the screen. The monitor is still in the storeroom. I thought that it was Kailash because he never liked my existence in that office.'

Dad's face became red. 'What are you saying?' he was confused and furious at the same time. 'How can someone abuse my daughter sitting in my office? Why didn't you tell me earlier?'

'I didn't want you to get stressed, Dad.' I almost wept while saying this. Two drops of hot tears rolled down my cheeks. Mom was standing as she was before. Her face was strong and cold with the shocks I was giving with my narration of the worst incidents of my life and the worst events of Dad's renowned and glorious company, MUSE. She was constantly looking at the terrace floor.

Dad came closer to me. 'Don't cry. Tell me what happened?' he was very softer now. As if he had melted entirely seeing me cry.

I quickly wiped my tears. 'That day, I had threatened them that if I catch the culprit that will be the end of his career. When I came back to my cabin, Kailash came and confessed that he stole the RAMs and sold them...'

'Kailash?' Dad was surprised again. His face muscle hardened again.

'Yes. I was shocked as I didn't expect the confession of the culprit so fast. He requested me not to tell anyone about this as it may end his career. I politely handled it when he said that he wasn't responsible for the tampering and all. In the evening, he surprised me more. He gave me money for those two RAMs and told me about his resignation.'

'As it was not in your hand, you asked him to resign to me?' Dad said.

'Yes.' I said, lowering my head. 'Sorry, Dad. I had no other options. I had thought that the problem is solved for the time being. It was very odd for him to resign suddenly for smuggling two RAMs when you don't even know about that.'

Dad hung his head and shook it a few times.

'Aarav told me that this job is Kailash's everything. It struck me hard. Why would a person break his own leg suddenly? One, if he suddenly doesn't need the job because of the money he made from smuggling for a year. Two, if he is tricked into this or blackmailed by someone to leave the job. I realized that something was seriously wrong. Aarav and I decided to check into the matter deeply.'

'Yeah. I know. Aarav will help you with everything. He is quite fond of you.' This came out of nowhere and shook me a bit for some seconds. His smiling face came to my mind automatically. I pushed it aside.

'What did you find out? That you hid from me?' Dad added the questions.

His hands were now behind him. His muscles tightened, and his forehead got so many unfamiliar curves. His eyes were cold.

'We checked Nehal's computer. His computer is the only one with a password in it. Aarav somehow guessed his password and cracked it.'

'Then?' his voice was getting cold.

'I hacked his computer.' I paused.

'What did you find?'

'A file. An Excel file with transaction details for a year. Almost seven lakhs. The customers are not ours.'

'And the seller's account? MUSE?' Dad asked. His face tightened so much that it could have blasted anytime.

'No.' I said.

'Nehal?' Mom spoke up in the middle.

'No, Mom. The seller is me.'

'WHAT?' they both shouted in shock.

'Yes, Dad and Mom. The seller's name is Farya Malik. And I am not the smuggler.'

'What are you saying?' This was Mom. Dad was probably not in a state to talk. I went to him and hold his hand, 'don't stress out Dad, plea...' I couldn't complete it. He suddenly fell on the chair.

'Dad!'

'I am okay. I am... just...' he put his index finger up to assure us that he was fine. Mom stood beside him. I sat near his feet on the terrace floor.

'I can't believe this. He knows your original name even before you joined MUSE. If the transaction is in your name, you will be blamed for the smuggle and not him. How clever!' Dad smirked.

Mom and I were quite shocked seeing him smirk like that.

'Very smart.' He said again. 'He double-crossed everyone. He double-crossed everything.'

'Dad, I promise I'll catch him and grab him by his collar to your feet.'

'I trust you, beta.' Dad said. 'Please leave me alone sometimes. Set dinner, Salma. I'm coming.'

We left Dad there. I climbed down first. Kaira sensed everything and remained silent. Mom came down after sometimes. She started setting dinner. Kaira started helping her. I stared at the blank wall of my room, sitting on my bed.

Once upon a time, this room was full of motivational posters. Now it's full of darkness. I never found myself in such an irritating situation in my life. I never found myself so hopeless and confused.

I dialed Haris and told him about everything that happened.

'It's good that your father took it quite well.' he said. 'Don't worry. He will understand you.'

'Can he trust my business ability anymore?'

'I think he should.' He said.

I took a deep breath. My eyes became moist.

'Are you free this weekend?' he asked.

'Yes. Why?'

'We are going to an important party.' He said. 'You will certainly feel better.'

'Okay.' I didn't drag it more.

xvi

Dear Diary,

I never thought that life would be complicated like this. I never thought that somebody can hate me so much. I never ever expected myself to land in this mess.

But it all happened. Quite soon.

It's just 2 and a half months I joined MUSE. Everything went wrong in between. On the contrary, if I haven't decided to join MUSE, Dad would never come to know this scam. But what the hell is happening? Who's the culprit? Nehal? Kailash? Amar? No. I don't think its Amar. But the things are lost from Ali's desk only. All the things that went missing were on Ali's account? How's this? Things go missing from Ali's account. Kailash takes the blame for it. Nehal meets strangers. It's more like a big scam chain.

Are they all connected? Are they doing it jointly? What if they are?

I had never been so broken in my entire life of twenty-four years. Not when my nanaji passed away. Not when I failed in History in class three. Not when I was cheated by Resham repeatedly. Not even when my Labrador died a year ago. I am really really confused and broken from inside. I can't show this, you know, because of Dad. I have to be strong.

In this two and a half months, I lost my permanent income. My daily routine has completely changed. My dressing sense has changed. I had fights with Haris. I stayed out of home for two nights. I fell in love. That's the most important part. Why have I to fall in love now?

Most specifically, why I fell in love with my secretary? This is another pain that I can't take anymore. Aarav and I have no future together. He's too young, even younger to me. He has his whole career waiting ahead to be fixed. He has an ailing mother to take care of.

And I really don't think that Aarav is behind all these. Haris talks about anything that comes to his mind. His theory is wrong.

I'll miss Haris. I was really sad when he had announced to me about that. But I didn't show him. He may get demotivated. But I already feel like crying for him.

God, help me!
Your's
Distressed
Ella.

I closed my diary. I wrote after two months. I rested my head back on the chair. I put my hands on the armrest and closed my eyes.

Aarav had confirmed to me in the morning that all the things that went missing were in Ali's account. Things were more complicated than I thought. My sixth sense was saying that I was pretty close to catch the culprit, the moron, the motherfucking fraud...

'Madam.' Sudhir's voice made me come to reality.

'Come in.' I said, sitting straight.

But he was not alone. 'Madam, this is Mr. Shukla. He wanted to meet you for some business talk.'

A man in a yellow T-shirt and blue jeans waited at the gate smiling. Sudhir was hesitating to let him in until I permit. I knew a person called Shukla. Dad had mentioned him a few times while talking about suppliers. He must be one of the suppliers.

'Come in, Shukla Ji.' I said. Aarav entered the cabin and scanned the two men carefully and gave me a brief nod. I knew what he meant.

'Have a seat, Mr. Shukla.' I showed him the chair across me.

'Madam, there's some work in the godown. I must leave.' Sudhir said.

'Sure.' I answered.

'Miss Malik.' Shukla's voice was very heavy and firm. But he was smiling all the time. That's a professional smile. Even I have learned about this smile by now. Shukla continued when I flashed the same smile at him.

'I am coming from C Technologies...'

'I know.' I cut him off. 'You are one of our top suppliers.'

'You are learning business, Miss Malik. That's good. That's very good.' He said. 'C Technologies is a growing company like MUSE, madam.' He paused again. 'In just three years we grew very well.'

Aarav and I exchanged a look that meant *"Iss Feku ko hatao re"*.

'We are trying to take bulk orders so that we focus on growing our business more strategically.' He said.

'Okay.'

'So, why MUSE is not interested in ordering in bulk? Do you know every other company in the market has agreed for bulk orders from us?' he asked. His question was simple but the drama he did before talking it out was very irritating.

'We don't have that much financial resource.' I answered. 'Bulk orders are a benefit for all, Mr. Shukla. For us as well. But we are not ready for it right now.'

'There's banks for loans, Miss Malik. You don't need an MBA to know that.' He laughed hysterically.

I tried to hold my patience. 'Mr. Shukla, MUSE doesn't run on debit. Sorry. We can't accept your request.'

'I was just suggesting.'

'Thanks for that.' I said.

'So, that's your final answer?' his face was turning pale.

'No, Shukla Ji.' I said very firmly. 'My answer is NO.'

My voice had raised a bit this time. That worked. He got up.

'Okay. Whatever you wish, Miss Malik. Business is not an easy thing. Just a piece of friendly advice.' He started walking to the door.

'I'll remember, Mr. Shukla.' I said. He didn't turn back. He left.

'That was quite bold.' Aarav said.

'I can't push everything to Dad. I have to handle a few on my own as well.' I uttered.

He nodded with a smile.

'Tell Sudhir not to send them to me again.' I said.

The next day was more dramatic. I was sitting in my cabin, thinking about Dad. He had turned very quiet since that night. It was not at all a good sign. I laid my head back on the chair and put my hands on the armrests. I closed my eyes and tried to think...

Who abused me? Who did the transaction for seven lakhs? Who...

My eyes shot open with a cracking sound of the door. Nehal was standing at the door.

'Aarav?' He raised his brows. 'I am searching for him since morning...'

'He's out for some bank work, Nehal. Tell me, what's it?' I said gently.

'Nothing, Ma'am... when will he come?'

'In an hour, probably.' I said.

'Okay. Thanks.' He left.

I dialed Aarav as soon as he left.

'Why is Nehal searching for you since morning?'

'I don't know, Ella.' He said.

Aarav ultimately started calling me by my name. That was making him closer to me. That was worrying me more about us. I didn't want to break my heart on my own again.

'Come soon.' I said.

'Yeah, okay.' He replied.

We hung up.

I went out of my cabin. Ali was on his desk. He was doing something on his computer. Sensing my presence, he looked up. He smiled at me briefly. I smiled back.

Nehal and Kailash were working on their respective desks. Amar was checking some notes. Maybe he was memorizing some important codes. I have seen him memorizing codes many times. Poor kid. All three of them looked at me at the same time.

'Anything needed, Ma'am?' Nehal asked me.

'No. I was getting bored in the cabin.'

'Oh, that happens in a closed place.' Ali said.

'Anyway, sorry to disturb you all. Please continue.'

'It's okay.' All of them said together.

I scanned everyone's screen and went to the watchman.

'Uncle,' I called him. He stood up instantly and made a salute.

'*Ji* madam.' He was a little surprised because I generally don't go to talk to him. 'You could have called me inside Ma'am. Why did you take the burden to come here?'

'You must stay here. You should not move from here. Okay?'

He bowed his head.

'From now onwards you will keep track of everyone going out and coming in. Okay?'

'That's my job.' He said.

'Which you don't do properly.'

He bowed his head again.

'Mind it. I want every detail with date and time. From now.'

'Is there any problem, Ma'am?'

'Yes.' I said. 'And I think you can help me solve it, uncle.'

He nodded. 'I will. Sorry, Ma'am for whatever happened. I hope it gets solved.'

I gave him a frustrating look. If he wasn't an uncle of my father's age, I would have fired him. Seriously. Though I still don't hold the authority to fire anyone.

'Ma'am, whatever it is. It will be solved. I'll be cautious. Nobody will be spared from my eyes.'

'It better be.' I walked inside the office.

xvii

I found my phone ringing when I came back to the cabin. I picked up the call.

'Hi.'

'Hi, Ella.' Haris said cheerfully.

'Lunch break?'

'Yes. Did you eat?' he asked like a caring sibling.

'Not yet. I'll eat soon after Aarav returns. He's out for some bank-related work.'

'Hmm.' He probably said that while sipping something. 'I hate office coffee. How's your one?'

'We have quality tea and coffee.' I jokingly said.

'Lol. I have to try once then. By the way, everything is okay at MUSE?'

'Why can't we talk about something else?'

'We can.' He said giggling. 'We surely can. My boss reviewed my application for transfer. He said that he would try his best.'

'That's great news.' I said smiling. Though the sadness of him leaving the country increased. 'Will you miss me?'

'I have not gone yet. Let me go first.' He laughed on the call.

'I'll miss you so much. For the first time, I am feeling the necessity of some more friends. I don't have a friend except you, Haris.'

'Hey, hey... I am not leaving the world.' He laughed again.

Aarav appeared on the door. Haris and I hung up. I sent him to meet Nehal as he was searching for him since the morning. When he came back, he had brought the worst news of my life...yet again!

Three more laptops were missing from Ali and Nehal's account. One of them belonged to office property of C Technologies!

My head started spinning. My eyes blurred. My hands were shaking vigorously. While Aarav was handling the situation with the staff, I dialed Haris.

'Ella, don't worry. Everything will be fine.' Haris told me on the phone. 'Just an hour ago everything was fine...'

'I know, Haris. But not now. I'm getting sick. I can't hold my breath.'

'Drink water, please.' He pleaded. 'I'm so worried about you.'

'Haris, they are smuggling right under my nose. What the fuck is happening?' I cried.

'Relax, Ella.'

'How can I relax? What will I tell Dad? That three laptops are missing again? What will I say to C Technologies? Shukla will kill us. He will make a huge fuss out of it. He needed a chance like this only.'

'You have to sort it out separately with Shukla. You can do it.' he tried his best to make me relaxed.

'And this Nehal? He was searching for Aarav to inform it. He didn't tell me even when I asked him about it.'

'He didn't tell you because he was afraid of you.' Haris tried to explain.

'The morons! The motherfucking dogs! I am going to the police now.'

'Ella, relax.'

'What relax? Why should I relax?' I shouted.

'Give the phone to Aarav.' He said.

'Why?' I said.

'Give him the phone, Ella, please.'

'Hold on.' I sat on the chair.

Aarav had come in the cabin meanwhile. He was sitting quietly behind me in his chair like he didn't exist.

I extended my hand to him. 'Haris wants to talk to you.' I said without looking at him. My head was burning now. He took the phone from my hand. I hold my head between my palms.

Aarav moved out of the room. I kept on sitting like that. What would I tell Dad? And why did Nehal waited to inform about the missing laptops to Aarav till he was back? Is there no value of me sitting here? My staff doesn't trust me? Or they don't rely on me? What's wrong with them?

'Ella,' Aarav came inside. 'Haris is right. We should not go to the police.'

'Shukla will surely go.' I said. 'He is always searching for a way to screw us. He will fuck us real bad.'

'Yeah. He can. He can go to any extent. But calling the police in MUSE will increase our problems only.'

I looked at him.

'We don't have a single clue or lead.'

'We have. The transaction file.' I said.

'What will you prove with that? It will create more problems for you, Ella.'

I didn't look at him anymore. My eyes were raining heavily. He came beside me.

He spoke up after sometimes, 'I think we should call Nehal here right now and question him about the Excel sheet.'

'Call him after an hour.' I said.

'Why are you crying, Ella? You are not that weak that you have to cry every time.' He walked by my side.

'What is happening, Aarav?' I broke down completely. I couldn't handle myself anymore. 'Why is it happening with me? What will I tell Dad?'

He held my hand gently and slowly pulled me up from the chair. 'Will you relax a bit?' his hands clasped mine tightly. I was still looking at the floor, crying. The thing that was bothering me the most was Dad's reaction about it that I was going to see soon.

'Ella,' he grabbed me closer to him, 'please don't cry. It's painful to see you crying like this.' His left hand came to my face. He tucked the free-flowing hair behind my ears. And the next thing he did - put me into an electric current shock. His thumb started wiping the tears. He wiped out every bit of tear from my eyes, cheeks, and neck. I kept on staring at his eyes directly. He kept staring at my eyes. Our looks were piercing through our eyes and reaching our souls. His lips were trembling as if he was trying to say something and failing constantly. His right hand was still clasped into mine. It was getting tighter with each passing moment.

His thumb wipes the last tear from my left cheek and rolled down to my lips. I didn't notice when we went too close to each other. I could feel his heartbeat now. I was pressed into his body. My heart under my black suit was trying hard to break everything apart and come out. My hands automatically went up. They rested on his shoulder. His hands moved to my waist. He grabbed me closer to him. I could smell his fragrance. No, not his perfume. But his original fragrance. It was mesmerizing. I couldn't hold myself anymore. I leaned towards him and closed my eyes. Our noses brushed against each other. Just when I thought that I would be kissing my secretary, I found an obstruction on my lips. My hair had set free again and fell on my lips. We set each other free in a moment.

What the fuck was happening right now?

I turned towards the washroom. I pushed the door open with the remaining energy I had. I closed the door behind me. I knew Aarav was standing as he was before. He was staring at me. I washed my face in the bathroom sink and wiped my face with a towel. I looked at my reflection in the bathroom mirror. It was awkward to look at my own face even. What was I going to do?

I decided to do one thing – to leave the washroom. I came out looking at the floor. Aarav was on his desk. I quickly scanned him. His eyes were confined on the laptop screen. He was pretending to work.

I grabbed my bag and put my hand inside. I grabbed a cigarette packet from inside and left for the open space attached to my cabin. Staring at the busy road down, I lit a cigarette. I inhaled deeply and closed my eyes. The moment flashed in my mind. My eyes shot open instantly.

Who's there? Down on the road?

I leaned over the railings to check him out. Well, it was Ali. He was talking to a man wearing a black hat. His nose and mouth were covered with a yellow checked scarf. He was wearing glasses. Basically, I couldn't recognize him at all. I tried to focus on the man. But he started walking already. Ali also came inside the office gate.

I took a long drag to the cigarette.

'Ella…' a very faint voice called me from behind. I didn't look back. I concentrated on the cigarette.

'I'm sorry.' He said. 'I shouldn't have made such moves. It's so…' his voice lost.

'It's okay. Aarav, I am equally responsible for whatever happened. Let's forget it.'

'No, you don't have any fault. Seriously, I am a jerk.'

I turned to face him. In the process, I smoked out right on his face. 'Sorry.' I quickly prompted.

'It's okay. You should not smoke though.'

I glared at him.

'No I mean I don't have a problem. Who am I to have a problem with your likes and dislikes? I mean that's bad for health… you obviously know…'

'Aarav. Stop.' I held my hand up. 'I am really fond of you. You are amazing. Seriously. Firstly, I got attracted to you because you look, I mean, not totally, but mostly, like my ex-boyfriend, Resham. But then I developed a feeling for you.' I looked away. I felt a hot sensation on my cheeks, ears, and nose. He stared at my face. I fixed my eyes on his; after some failed attempts.

'Aarav, that's okay… I mean, whatever happened. But I don't do my secretary… it's not right, Aarav. What will Dad feel about this? You are too young. You have your career, your dreams, your Mom and I don't want to be a … you know, right?'

'I understand.' He said. He was losing breath. As if he would weep now. 'I got your point. Your status and mine don't match.'

I turned back. My eyes were moist again. I hurt him. I hurt someone for the first time in my life. I rushed to the washroom again. I couldn't hold myself anymore. I broke down crying. I felt my heart aching. I felt the feeling that I didn't feel ever for anyone in my life. I was in love, for the first time in its purest form.

The whole day Aarav and I didn't even look at each other. However, that didn't affect our professional jobs. He called Nehal and asked about the Excel sheet. Nehal denied of anything like that. About today's lost laptop from his account, he said it was there yesterday when he left office. It's missing from this morning.

I had talked to Ali. Not in the cabin but on the terrace. I had asked him about the man he was talking down on the road.

'Ella, are you accusing me of the theft?' he narrowed an eye at me.

'No. I am just asking about the man.'

'He is a friend from school.' He said. 'He lives in Delhi. Came to Kolkata for a few days. He just wanted to meet me once.'

'Don't you know that you are not allowed to do personal works including meeting someone during the office hour?'

He lowered his head a bit. 'Sorry. Won't happen again.'

'Go to work.' I said.

He swiftly went out of the terrace gate. I stared at the sky. The sun had already gone for the day. There was still a bit of pink and orange in the sky. Darkness was hovering over the city. Over MUSE. Over me...

xviii

Nehal had informed everyone about the Excel file in the office. And everybody denied it. Though I didn't show it to anyone. Aarav brought out the accounts files of last year. The loophole was visible. A total loss of property of seven lakhs was clear. It happened since last year and Dad had kept on ignoring it ever since. A man who didn't even attend office properly will catch a thief like this? I had never thought that someone can have so much brain in real. We had to pay fifty thousand cash to Shukla for his lost laptop. We somehow had managed to stop him from going to the police. But other customers did what we were afraid of the most.

The customers almost tried to break in the office. Aarav and I could somehow stop them from calling the cops. The way the staff denied the Excel file, I had to force my mind to believe them. When I asked Kailash about them, he said that he did nothing except for smuggling those two RAMs. He said that he was already guilty of what he did and for that he is paying the price. Leaving MUSE was his punishment to himself.

On asking Ali, he said that he worked with proper attention and he didn't know anything about the smuggling. We had no evidence against Amar so we couldn't accuse him of anything. Well, after all, he also denied knowing anything at all.

In the process, I had to inform Dad. It was Friday. I called him in the office. He sensed that something was wrong. I had to brief everything to Dad in the office. He was completely silent while listening.

And the next moment was the worst I witnessed in my life.

Seeing your Dad collapse in front of your eyes, holding the left side of his chest is the worst thing you ever wish to witness. Everything got muted around me. I ran to Dad. He was already unconscious. I repeatedly called him.... 'Dad.... Dad.... Daaaaaaaad!' He didn't reply. Nor did he open his eyes.

They call it a heart attack.

Two hours later

I was sitting outside the OT. Aarav was beside me. He left for the hospital formalities only when Haris and Mom arrived. Kaira came directly from college. Her face was red – partly burned in the sun and partly red because of tears she had shed all the way. Haris had informed her. Seeing me, she started crying loudly. I hugged her tightly.

I never thought that Mom was so strong. She was managing everything silently as if going through a bad project phase, and soon it all would be over and she would be happily presenting it to everyone. She was once the managing director of an advertising agency. She left her job even before her marriage to my father. I heard her asking the doctor once, 'He will live, right?'

The doctor was silent. We cried even more.

After an hour, the doctor called us. Dad was transferred to the ICU. Nobody was allowed there. We sent Aarav to take care of the office. Before going, he had assured me that he would come to the hospital after office hour again. I didn't protest. I needed him.

'Mrs. Malik,' the doctor addressed Mom, who was quietly sitting on the chair across the doctor's table. Kaira and I were standing behind Mom. We didn't know what to come next. We didn't know if we could call 'Dad' ever. The doctor continued, 'he is not completely out of danger. It happened due to a tremendous shock. It is very natural but not at 56. Plus he is a diabetic patient. There's little risk. But don't worry.'

'He will live, right?' Mom asked the doctor again. Kaira wept louder this time. I hugged her tightly while my eyes rained heavily.

'We are trying our best Ma'am. Please be patient for 48 hours.' The doctor said professionally.

We left the doctor's cabin. We met Haris downstairs. He was talking to a nurse.

'Ella, everything will be fine.' He hugged me briefly. 'They don't have a particular medicine. So I'm going to another medical store for medicine.'

'You don't have to. You have to go to work.' I said, 'I can go for the medicines.'

'You don't have to worry much, okay? Uncle will be fine. Take care of aunty and Kaira. Be strong.' He said like a parent who delivers a string of instructions to his child before board exams. No matter the child is interested or not.

'Hmm.' I just nodded.

That day Aarav had come at night. We sent Haris home. I asked Aarav to drop Kaira and Mom at home. Mom obviously refused to go home, but I had to send her. I couldn't leave Kaira alone at home. She would go mad crying and think about the negatives.

I stayed in the hospital alone. The clock showed nine. The night fell silent around me. Even in hospital chaos, my mind went completely numb. Where did the three laptops go? How would we make up for fifty thousand cash that we paid to C Technologies? How would we ever manage to fulfil the gap created by those seven lakhs? What if the customers call the police for real?

I waited in the waiting room with five more people. A man in his mid-thirties sat there with a tensed face. From his conversation with the nurse, I could understand that his wife is in labour. She was going for a C-Section delivery soon. An old woman was accompanying the man. She was probably his mother or his wife's mother. At the extreme corner, there was a woman in her twenties sitting with a man of her age only. I didn't focus much on them. There was another man beside me. He was reading a magazine that he had pulled out hours ago from the stack that is put on the table in the middle of the waiting room. He was not talking to anyone. Nor he had any such interest to look at anyone even.

Mom and Haris had forced me to eat in the hospital canteen before leaving. Otherwise, I didn't feel like doing anything and would have kept thinking about the chronology of the events in my life. I cursed myself for calling Dad in the office. Why couldn't I shut my mouth and handle everything alone?

The Air Conditioner was not helping at all. They didn't even allow us to see Dad for once in the whole day. Already six hours had passed. I didn't know how he was. Was Dad in real pain? Was he even in his senses? What were they doing with my father? I wept again. Then I controlled myself.

I have to be strong. Very strong. I must. I have to take care of Mom and Kaira. I can't break down like this. Dad trusts me a lot. I have to fulfil his dream, his expectations. I must take Dad home. I have to...

'Miss Malik.' I found a nurse standing in front of me. 'You are Miss Malik, right? Patient party of ICU 3?'

'Yeah.' I stood up immediately. 'What happened?'

'Your patient gained consciousness. He's still serious, but he talked. He is searching for someone called Ella.'

'What?' I was so happy that I hugged the nurse. All the people in the waiting room looked at me once - even the magazine-man.

'Can I meet him?' I asked the nurse.

'Yes, you can. Come with me.' She said.

I followed her. I dialed Mom while climbing up the stairs.

'Mom... Dad is fine now. He talked.' I literally shouted at the top of my voice. 'Tell Kaira please.'

'I knew it. He can never leave us.' Mom started crying finally. I dialed Haris as well. He promised that he would come to meet Dad and me the day after and I should relax now.

I called Aarav too. He decided to come to the hospital. I asked him not to. But he said that he was already on the way to the hospital because he couldn't leave me alone there for the night.

'Ma'am, this is not a visiting hour. Please don't make a noise.' The nurse asked me professionally. I looked around. I never waited in a hospital so late at night. It's an entirely different world. The world of pain, hope and silence. A world - very different of MUSE. It's completely different than they show it in the flicks. It's much more serious.

We reached ICU 3. We pushed open a big glass door to reach the cabin. To reach Dad.

He was on the bed with so many machines connected to his body. I never saw so many cables and wires in my entire life even though I am a Computer Science Engineer and MUSE deals in Hardware mainly.

'Dad.' I called him softly.

He opened his palm and gestured me to come close to him. I put my hand in his. He held my hand tightly.

'Did you eat?' he asked, very softly.

'Yes.' I said. 'How are you feeling?'

'I am okay.' He said, smiling painfully. 'Don't stay here all day. Go to the office. Find out the person who is responsible for all these. I know you can do it, Ella.'

'Yes, Dad. I'll find him out. No matter what I have to go through for that. I can't spare the person who caused this to you.'

'Ella.' He called softly again, 'nobody caused anything, dear. I am firm always, but I'm getting old. That's why this heart attack.'

I got tears in my eyes.

'You will be fine, Dad. Everything should be fine... just like before.' It was more of consolation to myself.

He smiled and held my hand tighter. 'Where is my phone?' he asked.

'With Mom.'

'There's a phone number, saved with "Bose". Call him from my phone tomorrow, the first thing in the morning. Ask him to meet me in the hospital tomorrow evening.' Dad faced difficulty with talking.

'Who's he?'

'You will get to know.'

'Madam, please leave the patient alone now. You can't make him talk like this. Please, let him rest.' The nurse scolded me.

'I am okay. She is my daughter. Don't talk to her like this, please.' Dad said. Softly but firmly.

'Sir, you are not fine. You need to rest. Please, Ma'am.' She looked at me with a stern look after talking to Dad. 'This is an ICU.'

There are some people in the world whom you can never like. Their face resembles gunpoint every time they look at you. The nurse was one of them.

'I am downstairs, Dad. See you in the morning.' I said.

'Alone?' he asked. He had worry lines on his face.

'No.' I hesitated a bit. 'Aarav is coming. He had gone to drop Mom and Kaira at home. I informed them also. They will come in the morning. I have to stay here, Dad.'

'About Aarav...' Dad found difficulty to speak. My heart thumped a bit with the name of Aarav, 'he is a good guy.' He smiled after the sentence.

'Ma'am please...' the nurse stood between Dad and me.

'Okay, I'm leaving.' I stood up. 'Take care, Dad.' I said.

He slowly released my hand. He kept on staring at me. I also walked, staring back at him. The nurse escorted me to the waiting room. I could go alone, though. Maybe she didn't trust me.

'How's he?' Aarav asked as soon as he saw me. He was already sitting in the waiting room. Seeing me, he stood up.

'Strong and flexible.' I smiled. 'Dad is so strong, you know. I never thought that he would get a heart attack.'

'It was too much for him to take, Ella.' He said.

I sat down on a chair. He sat beside me on another chair.

'He couldn't take humiliations. What the customers did is expected after such mishaps. MUSE runs on reputation, and today it completely lost it.' He shook his head.

'It didn't,' I said. 'You know what Aarav, I will catch him, whoever he is.'

He nodded in support.

'Now it's just not about business, Aarav. It's personal.'

He smiled at me. 'It's very hard to think about the situation even.' He said.

We were silent for sometimes. We stood as we were.

He broke the ice. 'What did sir say? Did he talk properly?'

'Yes.' I said. 'He is talking fine and he didn't lose hope on me. He searched for me after gaining consciousness.'

'He loves you so much, Ella. I think he trusts you the most in the world.'

'I want my Dad home. Back.' I suppressed my tears. I hold my lips together to control my emotions.

'He will walk home. If I know him well I can guarantee about this.'

'You know what, from childhood, when people ask me what I wanted to do in life, my answer was very clear every time. "I want to be like Dad" I would always say with pride. I never imagined how it would be to become a person like "Dad". I never knew it's so tough. I never knew how it feels to be "like Dad". But now, I know. I know what it is. I know how it is. Being a Dad is not an easy task.'

He smiled at me, 'You are fortunate to have a Dad like him. And he is luckier to have a daughter like you.'

I kept quiet.

'It's time, Ella. Show the so-called men's world that you are your Daddy's daughter.'

'Right. It's time.' I nodded.

'And your Watson is always there for you.' He said.

'Yaay... I became a father... Oh My God!!!'

We were puzzled for sometimes. Then we gathered the situation. The man in his mid-thirties became a father finally. His wife delivered a baby boy. It was his first reaction to that. Aarav and I shared an awkward look. The magazine man just smiled at us, awkwardly, as well. The man and woman in mid-twenties – well, they were nowhere to be seen. They must have left.

We didn't sleep the whole night. We discussed different ways to catch the culprit. We thought about different plans to lift MUSE from its distressed zone. We talked about his mother. We talked about his life in Delhi before he moved to Kolkata with his mother. We talked a lot.

It was 6 AM and he had to leave. He had to go home, cook, help his mother with her diet and medicines and leave for MUSE.

'What is the first thing you would do after these all ends?' he asked, getting up the chair.

'I'll think about it. I'll do something extraordinary.'

'Good luck with that.' He said, smiling.

'What will you do when all these ends?'

'I'll join college for MBA only if MUSE let me go.' He said. 'But neither you nor sir wants me to go… so, I'll stay in the company only being a happy secretary of a great boss.'

'Which of your bosses?' I smiled, looking at him.

He smiled in return. 'Now I see they are pretty much same. But obviously, the younger one is greater.'

I smiled at him. 'You signed a three years contract with MUSE.'

'I know. But that's not the reason I am not leaving. There's another reason for staying in MUSE. And you know it well.' He smiled, looking down. 'I can't leave you alone in the sea. Even great bosses need great secretaries.'

I stared at his face. He stared at mine.

'Bye. Take care. See you soon.' He said, walking towards the gate of the waiting room. It was totally empty now.

'Aarav.' I called him from behind. He looked back.

'We should have kissed that day.' He stared at me quietly for sometimes. Then he smiled, biting his lower lips.

'I think you don't do your staff.'

I looked down.

'I also decided not to do my boss.' He pushed the gate and went out. I looked at him, deceasing away. Going far away from me. I stared for a long time blankly.

xix

'You are so unpredictable, Ella.' Haris said, taking a sip of coffee. I drank my tea in a go. It was already cold, and there's no point in sipping it. He continued, 'Firstly, you fell in love with him. Now when he has the same feeling for you, you told him one of your creepy dialogues.' He mimicked me, 'I don't do my staff.'

'He said that he doesn't do his bosses too.' I snapped back.

'Oh, for fuck's sake, please stop your shits. Stop shitting everywhere and try to clean whatever you spread at first.' He said.

'Why are you so pissed off?'

'Because the person who always gives me relationship advice is now screwing herself. What will you do when I am gone?'

'It's very awkward to date him, being his boss, Haris. Please understand. Can you date your boss?'

'For your kind information, my boss is a 50 years old man with an ugly mustache that he never cleans, I'm sure, and eats making an annoying sound. Only he pays me well and thinks I deserve an international transfer; that's why I am there. I have no intention to date him.'

'Cut the crap. Just imagine if he was not a man but a lady. Would you date him, I mean her?'

He thought for sometimes holding his cup. 'No.' he said. Then he added. 'But Aarav is not your boss. He is your staff. You can make a move on him, c'mon.'

'I don't want to talk to you regarding this.' I got up.

'Pay the bills at least.' He giggled.

'You are a piece of shit.'

'Yes, an expensive one.'

We paid for the coffee and the tea and left the hospital canteen. We already met Dad once. Haris would go to the office now, and I would visit Dad again. It was 10:30. The visiting hour ends at 11 AM. So I escorted him to the hospital gate and went upstairs to meet Dad. Mom and Kaira already met and they were downstairs. I met my maternal uncle in Dad's cabin. He was talking to Dad. Seeing me, he smiled and hugged me.

'Ella dear, if you need anything, you can come to your *mamaji* without any hesitation.' He said.

Seriously? Now that my Dad is bedridden, you came here to guide me. I'm no kid. I thought in my mind. What I said to him was, 'Yes, *mamaji*. Sure.'

Mamaji left. The nurse showed me the clock - fifteen minutes to eleven. I nodded, smiling at her.

Bitch with an AK-47 face!

'She is doing her job dear. Let her do it.' Dad smiled at me, probably, after reading my face. Dads know it all!

I smiled at him.

'Did you call Bose?' he asked.

'Yes, Dad.' I said. 'Who is he, by the way?'

I asked, putting a hand on his head to comfort him.

'Lawyer.' He said.

'Lawyer?' I was surprised. 'Why do you need a lawyer at the hospital?'

'I told your Mom already. I am taking a big decision. You'll come to know.' He smiled.

'What are you going to do?' I was completely serious by now.

'Ma'am, please, don't make the patient talk much. Please, Ma'am. I beg of you.' The nurse shouted at me.

Bloody overacting!

'Please, go out, Ma'am.'

'Ella, go to the office, *beta*.' Dad said to me. 'What will you do here? I am fine.'

'I'll come in the evening.' I said to Dad, kissing his forehead.

The nurse stared at me all the while. I went home with Mom and Kaira. I was in the hospital since the day before. I was stinking. I took a long bath.

Mom asked me to go to the office after lunch. I was having lunch with my family on a weekday after a long time. It felt good but didn't feel complete because of Dad's absence. I just prayed for his safe return home.

When I was fifteen years old, Dad had gone for a business trip with Mr. Malhotra to the UK to help him in his business deals. I didn't react to Dad's absence for fifty-five days. But when he called us before boarding the flight back to India, I couldn't sleep the whole night. All the while he was in the flight, I stayed awake praying for his safe return. I was worried about him. So many thoughts came to my mind that night. What if Dad doesn't return? What if something happens to him on the flight? What if he doesn't ask for me the first thing after landing here? What if he has lost attachment with us already because he didn't talk to us properly from the UK.

I had cried even while Mom and Kaira were sleeping sound. In the morning, Mom had driven us to the airport to pick Dad and Malhotra up. The first thing that Dad had said after coming out of the airport terminus was "Ella, how are you, *beta*? You are looking thinner."

That was Dad's first and last trip away from us and without us.

Today, sitting in the dining table with my mother and sister, I felt the same I felt that night. Tears rolled down my eyes.

'Ella...' Mom's voice came faintly seeing me crying.

'Mom, Dad will be okay, right?' I broke down crying. 'I don't want to be an orphan...' I chocked. Seeing me, Kaira also started crying.

'What are you girls doing? He is....okay...he's fine.' Mom was losing words. 'He will come back home in a few days, *Insha'Allah.*'

We went on weeping.

'Why is he calling for the lawyer?' I asked Mom.

'What? Lawyer?' Kaira was absolutely unaware of the whole thing.

'It's his personal work. He has a plan.' Mom said.

'Why is he hurrying up to meet the lawyer, Mom?' I said.

'Stop predicting the bad, Ella. It's nothing serious.' Mom put a hand on my head. 'Kaira, you too, please eat.'

We were not in a mood to eat anymore. But we had to eat as Mom instructed us to finish the food quietly. Even she didn't eat properly.

I went to the office. I found Aarav very busy updating the monthly report.

'Did we make any profit?' I asked him after sitting on my chair.

'Hmm.' He said.

'We made a profit after all these?' I smirked.

'Hmm.'

'We should hire a professional accountant. Then you don't have to do these extra jobs.' I said without looking at him. 'I don't know how Dad maintained everything with just a few people.'

'Hmm.'

I turned to him. 'What happened to you?' I asked.

'Nothing.' he said without looking at me. He was doing his job with concentration. Okay, that's what he pretended to do.

'No. Something is there, tell me.' I walked to him. He didn't say anything.

'I think I am audible to you, Aarav.'

He didn't react. He was quietly working on the laptop, and so, my temper shot up. I shut the screen of the laptop. It happened so quickly that I literally slammed the screen on his hands that were on the keyboards of the laptop. He took his hands out.

'What happened?' I asked again.

'Can you move a bit? So that I can get up from this bloody chair?'

Language!

'Okay.' I pulled myself away a bit. He left his chair and stood in front of me. He took a deep breath. Then he wiped out sweat from his forehead. I looked at the AC. It was on, and the temperature showed 22 degrees. I looked at him again. He was brushing his curly hairs from his forehead with his long fingers.

'What is this drama for?'

'Do you think this is drama?' he shouted at me. 'I am getting sweat in an air-conditioned room, and you think its drama? Miss Malik, do you even know what you want?'

'What are you talking about?' I was puzzled.

'Ella, your father is in the hospital. He got a heart attack at 56 and still in the ICU. And you are still not serious about catching the culprit?'

'What's wrong with you?' I said. 'I am quite serious about it. But I can't take any decision right now. Let Dad come home. I will plan anything out to find out the truth.'

'It will be so late. He ran the company for twenty years flawlessly with his old school ideas, and you got punctured in just twenty days. Did you realize it?' He said.

I sat on my chair. 'What should I do now?'

'First, tell me, you want to solve this problem or not?' he asked, leaning on my table in front of me.

'Yes. But in case I find out that one of my father's staff is the culprit I will have nothing to do except reporting it to Dad. Because he is the only person who will decide what to do next. And I don't want him to get more shock. He is still not out of danger.' I said softly.

He took a deep breath. 'We will sort it out. At least plan out something.' He said.

'Aarav, I know I am not a responsible and deserving boss, but I am trying to be one. I am trying hard to take control of everything.'

He nodded. 'You are the most undeserving boss MUSE ever had.' And the next moment he laughed. 'But the undeserving one can make a big difference if she is the chosen one. And don't forget that out of so many options, you are chosen to handle this empire.'

I smiled painfully. 'After my arrival, MUSE is facing more smuggles, more financial problems, and more misunderstandings.'

'That's why you are undeserving.'

I kept quiet.

'But you are also the chosen one. So focus on that.'

'Aarav, MUSE is my Dad's property and my responsibility. That's why I am so troubled about it. Why are you troubled?'

'Because I have three years contact with MUSE and if MUSE goes down, who will pay my salary?'

I looked at him instantly. He laughed on my face.

'You are an assh...'

He continued laughing. I stared at his face.

'I have no reason to get troubled. As I have nothing productive to do here, I got myself involved in this.' He said laughing, 'are you satisfied with the answer?'

'No.'

He smiled again and walked out of the cabin. I also got a smile on my face. Unknowingly I even chuckled a bit.

Aarav is amazing!

On returning home that night, I found my *Dadi* in the house. I knew she would come. I felt good seeing her. Even Mom got some courage. She was smiling, finally.

'Seems like you have jumped few years ahead of time in just a few months.' *Dadi* said to me, hugging me tightly. 'I can see the marks of responsibility on your face, my munchkin.' She smiled, kissing my forehead.

'Who took you here?' I asked as I knew that she couldn't come alone.

'Shadab beta took me here. He wanted to meet you as well. But he had to go for some personal reasons. I don't know what he's up to.' She said. 'He is not interested in studies, not even in sports, not even in handling the business.'

'It's okay. Everyone is not the same.' I said to her.

'Hmm. You talk like your father, Ella.' She said.

I smiled.

'You know what, Shadab's Mom is not happy about you joining MUSE.' She said. 'But he is very happy for you. He is foolish but good at heart.'

'I know, *Dadi*.'

'Business is not everyone's cup of tea. Shadab's father couldn't ever do good in business. He finally had left everything behind and joined a 9 to 5 job. He is my son too. But see, there's a lot of difference between your Dad and Shadab's Dad.'

I nodded.

'I'm proud of you. Not only because you joined MUSE. Also, because you broke a stereotype of our family. You are the first woman in our family to become a "torch-bearer" in a family business.' She put a hand on my head. 'Family business is always passed to the sons of the house. Not daughters, ever.'

'I'm lucky.' I smiled. For a moment, a feeling of huge proudness filled my heart and soul. I felt happy and satisfied with myself. I wanted to hug myself. And pat my back, saying, *'well done, Ella.'*

XX

Kaira was at home alone. Mom and *Dadi* had gone to see Dad. They would return anytime.

'You didn't go to the hospital?' Kaira asked me.

'They won't allow so many people and Dad wants me to be in the office. So, I didn't go today.'

'How's Aarav?' She asked.

I was a little surprised by her question. Why would she ask about him all of a sudden in this situation?

'He's fine.'

She nodded. I waited for her to say something, but she didn't.

I went for a bath. Kaira gave me hot Maggi noodles to eat. I sat down. She was having tea. She generally doesn't like tea. She probably had made it for Mom, me and *Dadi* as we were returning home late and missed evening snacks.

'I miss Dad.' She said. 'He always shouts on me, saying that I would fail in my masters if I don't take it seriously.' She laughed at the end. Then I saw two drops of tears in her eyes. 'Dad is getting old, really.' She added. 'I always thought that my father would never get old no matter what. But like others, my father is also getting old.'

It is indeed painful to see our parents growing old. We want our parents to stay young just like that ailing person wanted the last leaf to remain on the tree.

'Kaira, he is getting fine.' I said, trying to hold myself like a big sister.

'Your greatest fear is to lose MUSE. My greatest fear is to lose a Dad.' She wept. 'They are not the same.'

'How do you know about my fear?' I asked.

She kept quiet.

'Kaira, you are not a grownup until you have more than one fear. I don't discuss my fears. But that doesn't mean I don't have more than one fears. You must know it all today.' I spoke up. 'I have a fear of losing MUSE's reputation. I am afraid of going on loss and filling the gap of seven lakhs, including recent loss. I have a fear of Dad's life. I have a fear of Dad losing trust in me. I am afraid of...' I couldn't finish. As the doorbell rang, Kaira quickly wiped her tears.

Mom was there with a man. He was wearing a white shirt and a black coat. Who wears a black coat in summer?

Unless he is a lawyer... He is the lawyer.

'Mr. Bose?' The name suddenly escaped my mouth.

'Oh, dear. You know me.' The man said. Though I had talked to him on the phone, his voice seemed familiar.

Mom smiled. 'Ella, he is Mr. Bose, our lawyer. And Mr. Boss, she is Ella, I mean, Farya Malik, my elder daughter and she is Kaira Malik, my younger one.'

'Your daughters are sweet, Mrs. Malik. Nice to meet you, girls.' Mr. Bose said to us.

He was in his mid-thirties. He has a sharp face that looked intelligent. He smiled at me, sitting on the sofa.

Kaira served him tea, chocolate, and biscuits.

Mom informed me that *Dadi* had decided to stay in the hospital with Dad overnight. What she would do alone in the waiting room was out of the question. *Dadi* has her own mood.

Mom sat beside me on the sofa while Mr. Boss sat across us on the other sofa.

'So, Miss Malik, I am here to brief you about the decision that your parents, especially, your father, Mr. Malik has taken in his bedridden condition.'

I was puzzled. I looked at Mom. Mom pointed at Mr. Bose. I looked at him.

'Miss Malik, your father's company, Modernus Enterprise is getting transferred to your name by your father's wish.'

'WHAT?'

'Yes, Miss Malik, let me complete.' He smiled.

I looked at Mom, surprised. Mom smiled plainly at me. Her eyes were glittering, though.

'As your father thinks that he can't run the company anymore, he wants you to be the new owner and CEO of Modernus Enterprise.'

'What is he saying Mom?' I got up from my place.

'He is saying the right thing, Ella.' Mom said. 'Your father wants that, and he discussed it with me in the morning. I agree with him in this.'

The lawyer sat quietly, sipping tea.

'But he could have talked to me once. How can I...'

'Why can't you, Ella?' Kaira spoke up. 'You are the only person who can handle it after Dad. And about your fears, its time to win over them. Ella, you should be happy that Dad chose you for this. He is doing something great for you for the first time. As a matter of fact, he is doing something great for all of us.'

'Kaira, you don't understand.' I snapped at her. 'Mom,' I sat beside her, 'what would grandma say? What would the rest of the family say? Why is Dad making me the owner? What's Dad and your future? Legally, the company is mine, and when I get married, my husband can also claim the company as my counterpart. Do you understand, Mom?'

'Yes, Ella. Your Dad understands the best.' She said.

'Miss Malik,' the lawyer spoke up now. 'Your father has made a clause. You should give 30% of the annual income for your parents. You should also give 15% of the yearly income to your sister, Miss Kaira Malik and 5% to the charity that is run by MUSE.'

'We have a charity organization?' I looked at Mom.

She nodded. 'Yes, even I didn't know it.'

Mr. Bose smiled. 'Mr. Malik is a very peculiar man, indeed. He does a lot of things without letting a soul know about it. I have never seen such a genius, a kind and nice man in my life.'

'His kindness is his main weakness.' Mom smiled.

'The rest of the income, that is, 50%, is the company's', said Mr. Bose. 'Yours.'

'Dad could have done all these after coming back from the hospital. What's so urgent?'

Everyone was quiet.

'Why does he think that he would never recover?' My voice became heavy.

There was still pin drop silence.

'Miss Farya, I think he is doing the right thing. As his legal advisor, I can say that he is a genius, and he proved it again by doing this.'

I kept quiet now.

'Ella,' Mom put a hand on my head, 'please.'

'What I have to do, Mr. Bose?' I asked.

'Well, I almost prepared the papers. It's not so easy to prepare everything in such short notice.' He smiled. 'You have to sign a few papers on Monday morning.'

'Okay.' I said. 'Mom, can I go to my room?' I stressed out.

'Sure, beta.' She said.

I went to my room and closed the door from inside. I generally don't lock my door but I did that day.

I pulled out a cigarette from a secret shelf in the wardrobe and lit it. I sat on my bed and smoked it hard. Like, really hard. I almost swallowed the fire. My lungs burned for a minute. I rubbed my chest vigorously.

I grabbed my phone and dialed Haris after 2 long puffs and a long burn. He picked up instantly.

'Hey, how's uncle?' the first thing he asked turned me more tensed.

'Haris, I am in trouble.' I spoke up.

'What did Aarav do now?'

'Oh.' I chuckled even in this condition. 'It's not him. It's Dad.'

'What happened?' he was serious now.

'Haris, let me complete, *yaar*.'

'Oh, sorry.'

'Dad is transferring the company to me. I am going to be the new owner and CEO of MUSE. He added a few clauses as well.'

'WHAT?' he was gasping like a goldfish, I knew.

'What are you saying?' he paused again. 'That's GREATTTT.' He shouted finally.

'I'm confused. I am not ready for this.' I said.

'Hey, don't be mad, okay? It's all right. What are the clauses, by the way?'

I explained everything to him that Mr. Bose has told me. He listened to me carefully.

'I knew uncle is freakish but he turned out to be completely insane,' he laughed, 'in a good way though.'

I smoked again.

'Are you smoking? Where are you?' he asked.

'At home. In my room.' I said.

'Bold, eh? Why not? The new boss of MUSE cannot smoke at home even? Surely she can.' He laughed loudly.

'Your enthusiasm is a little more than expected.'

'I am happy, super happy, actually. I am just amazed. My best friend is now a CEO, huh?' he giggled. 'I wanna hug you tight, dear lady.'

'You are overacting.'

'Maybe. But why not?'

He was actually very happy. He was happy like this when I topped in my school in the tenth Board exam. Haris is crazy, but the most supportive friend one can have.

I finally smiled. I wanted to talk to Aarav too. But I was not supposed to disclose this to any office staff soon.

The next day was Sunday. I went to meet Dad in the morning. He was still in the ICU. The nurse didn't let me enter the ICU. I just saw him sleeping from the closed door. I went to meet the doctor.

'Sir, is he not well?' I asked. 'I mean, is he out of danger?'

The doctor smiled at me.

'Miss Malik, he is recovering. He is not completely out of danger. He is talking a lot with visitors. Please stop visiting him like this. Especially, he is talking with you so much. The nurse was complaining. And please, take your grandmother home.'

I lowered my head.

'Miss Malik, your Dad will be fine and walk home. I guarantee you. Please leave him to rest in isolation.'

I nodded. I left his cabin. *Dadi* was in the waiting room. She hugged me, seeing me.

'*Dadi*, you don't have to be here. He will be fine. Let's go home, please.'

She agreed. We took a cab. All the while, she was lost. I tried to console her in every way while I needed it the most.

Why was Dad so desperate to leave the company to me? Was he not well enough to return home? Was he aware of something terrible?

I told *Dadi* about the company-transfer. She said that it was a good decision. She also wanted that. However, other members of my family may get a shock after coming across such news. I knew who she was pointing too.

Above everything, my mind didn't let me rest. I didn't sleep for 3 nights.

I came back home at 12 pm and took a long bath. *Dadi* made some porridge for us. I was enjoying it sitting on my bed in my room when Haris came. He was fully dressed up. He was insisting on me going to a party with him.

'I already had told you about it.'

'I am not going. Not after all these.'

'It's nothing big, Ella. Get out of these for a few hours. I have talked to aunty and *Dadi* as well. They also think you should go.'

'But...'

'Get up.' he said. 'It's not even a party like you are thinking. Just a get-together with our college friends over lunch.' he pulled me up of the bed with my hand.

'But I don't have a dress...' I sat on the bed again.

Haris was wearing black pants and a white shirt tucked in neatly. The sleeves were folded up to his elbows. The shoes he came wearing were from Gucci, and the wristwatch was from Titan. It was given by me to him on one of his birthdays.

'It's not a fashion show.' He said.

'Who's saying?' I scanned him from top to bottom.

'What?' He said. 'I normally look like this. It's my go-to look.'

'Seriously? Gucci shoes?'

'Okay. That's an addition. Except that, everything is too old.'

I still sat on the bed, making a sad face. 'I don't feel like getting up and dressed... and do makeup...'

'Okay, I'll do your makeup. Happy? Go, please. Get dressed.' Haris pulled me up again.

'Don't you remember the last time what disaster you did to my face in the name of makeup?'

He laughed. 'I really like to experiment with your face and hair and...'

'You are still not ready?' mom asked me, entering my room. Haris had to stop bragging about his makeup skills.

'Mom, I'm not in the mood to go anywhere.' I complained.

'You will feel good, Ella. You have to get out of this box.' She said, brushing my hair with her fingers. 'Your *Dadi* was saying that you, completely, filled yourself with MUSE and family. You have a life too, Ella. You are too young to get tangled in all these. Please, go. Enjoy a day out.'

'Right. Let's go. I'm hungry.' Haris uttered.

I gave him a 'die-of-eating' look and opened my wardrobe. He showed me a middle finger in a way that Mom couldn't see and followed Mom out of the room.

I chose a short black dress with lacy sleeves. I wore the dress and started combing my hair. The hospital didn't even let me meet Dad once. If he was serious, they would have called. No call came as well. I started missing Dad a lot. While I was applying the lipstick, I cried.

An hour later we were at a five-star hotel's restaurant to have lunch with our friends. Our friends mean – Jayanti, Shikha, Aliya, Kritika, Mahi, Roshan, and Amal. They all were in college with us. Everyone's a Computer Science Engineer. Except for Jayanti, everyone is in corporate jobs. Jayanti was still studying interior design in Mumbai. Yes, she had changed her plan after B.Tech. Aliya was already married after college. So, she started the conversation with the name of her 'rich and handsome' husband.

Everything was tolerable until I saw someone approaching our table. I hadn't noticed that there was an extra chair kept for someone else.

'Did you know about him joining us?' I fired at Haris.

'Yes.' He said, trying to avoid eye-contact and focus on his prawn cutlet.

Jayanti hugged the person tightly. Aliya and Kritika continued to get awestruck by his appearance just like old college days. The guys greeted each other in their typical "dude style".

'Hey, Haris.' He approached Haris extending a hand. Haris quickly rubbed his hands with a tissue paper and shook hands with him. 'Hello, Resham.' They exchanged a smile. This was too much to take for the day.

'Hi, Ella. How are you?' Resham sat beside me on the empty chair. Every pair of eyes were glancing at us. Except for Haris though. He was busy eating.

'I am fine.' I somehow uttered.

'I'm glad to see you here.' Resham said, 'I didn't expect you here. By the way, you look amazing. Mature and pretty.'

I gave a killer-look at Haris. He focused on the prawn.

'I didn't know you are coming. Otherwise, your expectation would have been true.' I said, grabbing a sharp fork.

'So, you guys meeting for the first time after... you know what I mean...breakup?' Jayanti giggled.

I kept quiet.

'Friendship never ends.' Aliya commented. 'They can be friends now.'

'Right.' Everyone said in unison except for Resham and Haris.

I stabbed a chicken breast and put some in my mouth.

'How's work, Haris?' Resham asked.

'It's more than expected.' Haris giggled. 'How's yours?'

'Good.' He said. 'My boss is the best one in the world. She is just amazing. Plus, there's a regular hike.' He paused. 'I am pleased with my life.'

Fake.

'I have heard that you joined your Dad's business.' Amal looked at me.

'Yes.' I said.

'Oh, you left the job?' Resham turned to me.

'Yes.'

'Why?'

'Because I was not "pleased" with my life there.' I looked straight at him.

He had changed a bit. He looked more presentable now. He brushed his hair once with his fingers and nodded.

'It's so good to have Dad's company.' Aliya said. 'Your own company. Wow!'

'Ella is going to be the CEO soon.' Haris announced. I didn't want him to talk so much. Seriously. I was angry.

'Wow!' Resham said. 'How splendid it is to sit in a company, becoming CEO at twenty-four, and enjoying the bossy life. I have always thought that you would be a self-made person. But you chose the privilege to jump on your father's ready-made business.' He laughed at the end. 'But that's clever.'

My brain shot up. It crossed its tolerance level. I dropped the fork and spoon on the table. Everyone looked at me. I left the chair and walked towards the restroom.

'Ella.' I heard Haris' voice. 'Don't mind him. He's always a dick.'

I stopped outside the restroom. 'Why didn't you tell me about him?'

'I wasn't sure about him. I thought he wouldn't come.'

'You "thought"?'

'Okay, sorry. But he can't spoil the day like this.'

'Who is he to talk about my father's company? Who is he to talk about my choices?' I shouted.

'Relax...'

'Oh, you are angry, I see.' Resham came there, making me fume more. 'Take it easy, lady. We are still friends.'

'Fuck you, Resham. We can never be friends. And your sense of humour still sucks.' I cried aloud.

He laughed. That made me fume more. 'You have already started acting like a maniac boss, Ella.' He said, laughing hysterically.

'Hey, dude, enough.' Haris stood between us. 'She is more capable of doing something productive in her life than you, okay? At least, she is not a fake like you. Just stay away from her. She is not a maniac, FYI. And FYI again, she is not single anymore. So, stop digging on her whenever you get a chance. And work on your jokes and humour, please. You seriously need to work on it.'

Resham was surprised. So was I – hearing that I wasn't single.

We didn't wait anymore. We grabbed our belongings and paid our bills and left. Actually, nobody cared for us anymore there. Nobody even stopped us. Everything was a competition now, and friendship had lost somewhere. It is true- friendship changes its definition with time.

Finally, on Monday morning, in the presence of Mom, Kaira, *Dadi*, and Mr. Bose, I signed the papers. I was officially the owner and CEO of MUSE. All the employees were informed through a video conference by Dad from the hospital.

Things happened pretty fast. I had asked Dad why he did this. He just smiled and said, 'for the betterment of MUSE.'

At night, Mom came to my room. She had a smile on her face. I was going through some important files that Aarav had mailed me. She sat beside me on the bed and took my laptop away.

'I want to talk.' She said, putting the laptop away from me. 'I hope I'm not disturbing you much.'

'Yes, you just put my laptop away.' I said.

She laughed. I joined her with mild laughter.

'I am happy for you.' She said. 'It's like I won for the first time in life. My daughter is a deserving CEO, no doubt.'

I stared at her quietly.

She continued, 'Ella, passing on a family business to a daughter is a tough decision. I'm glad about your father's decision today. For this family, Shadab is thought to be everything. Since his birth, he is given utmost importance, love, care and affection. So that he can handle the family's heritage, business, and every other thing. He is after all the only son this family has.' She paused. 'Like this, many deserving daughters are betrayed in this society. We always tend to ignore our daughters saying that she will go to some other house and there she can claim everything. However, that "other house" only thinks about their son just like we think about our son, Shadab. Ultimately, the daughter or the daughter-in-law is always left out. She is always ignored.'

'Mom, why did you leave the job before marriage?'

She smiled. 'That's an old story.'

'Dad would never ask you to leave the job.'

'When my marriage got fixed to your Dad, my father had told me to quit working. He had asked me to focus on the family. He thought that I couldn't handle both together. Maybe he was right. I am not as dynamic as you, Ella.' She said.

I kept quiet.

'You are so dynamic. A multitasker, I must say.' She continued, 'You are intelligent, loving and caring. You are developing a sense of responsibility that a privileged girl of your age generally doesn't. Either they think about getting married, or they want more money to buy makeups and go for foreign tours. I'm glad to see that my daughter chose differently. I know how important MBA was for you. You always wanted to go to a foreign university. I feel sad for you sometimes, Ella.

Then again, I convince my mind that just a handful of a daughter has a mindset like you. Our country needs more daughters like you. This is the real women empowerment.'

I hugged her tightly. She brushed my hair gently.

'Always remember one thing, no matter how high you fly, never forget to look down. After your flight, you have to land on the ground only.'

'I'll always remember, Mom.'

'In business, you will always see negativities and inhumanities. But never lose your humanity.' She added.

I nodded.

She put a hand on my head and smiled. She was happy. What could be more important than her happiness? I felt happy too.

xxi

"So how do you feel when you become the CEO of your father's company overnight? Oh well, you are the owner... Fuck!"

I wrote this in my diary and threw it in the wardrobe. I removed the towel that I was wrapped in after the shower. Writing a diary in a towel felt sexy. I saw my naked reflection in the mirror.

The mirror is of my height. I grew up, it didn't. It was fixed in my room by Mom when I was eight. Well, they didn't actually buy it for me. They didn't even buy it. A carpenter had promised to build a small wardrobe in Mom's room for her cosmetics. Well, she owns a lot of cosmetics but never uses them properly. The carpenter never delivered that wardrobe even after taking money from Dad. In return, he had delivered a huge mirror that some other customer had refused to take.

Not getting a place to put that mirror up, my mother fixed it up in my room. Initially, I loved it. I could see my whole reflection in it. I would dance the whole day in front of it, wearing Mom's drapes. Later, it became so boring.

Did I lose weight? I glanced at my naked reflection again. Maybe I did lose some kilos. But it was fine. I am thin. I still have a flat belly, thank God! Many of my friends envied me in college for that belly.

Though they made fun of my small breasts. But that's fine. They are not the CEO of a successful company... well, it lost its reputation for now, but it will be fine... – I thought.

I was the CEO now. Your breast size doesn't matter. Your weight doesn't matter and your...whatever, nothing matters to become a CEO.

I realized that my mind was blabbering. My phone rang up. I turned towards it. It was lying on the bed all the while.

MUSE was closed on Monday. It was Dad's last day as the owner and CEO, so he had declared a holiday. Today was Tuesday. My first day as the CEO. God, I got Goosebumps!

'Hello, Aarav.' I picked the call up.

'Hi, Madam CEO.' His voice was cheerful.

'Hi. How can I help you?' I playfully said.

'I don't need help. But I am always there to help you with anything you need.' He said, 'After all, you are my new boss.'

I laughed.

'Will you do me a favor?' I asked after sometimes when he didn't say anything.

'Sure.' He instantly said.

'Will you teach me driving? I don't like sitting on a stranger's side to learn driving.'

'Haris could do that.' He prompted.

'No. He will shout on me a lot.' I said, 'Same with Mom.'

'Okay. I will.' He said.

'Thanks. Take a cab and come home. I'll go with you today in our car.'

He kept quiet sometimes. Then he responded, 'sure.'

'Aarav,' I called him, 'I still like you a lot.'

'I know.' He quickly said.

There was silence for sometimes on both sides.

'I think I should get ready.' He said, breaking the iceberg that formed between us.

The call got disconnected before I could say anything.

What should I wear? I thought for sometimes and pulled out matching red lingerie that I had bought a year ago and never wore. I thought of starting everything fresh. Why not new lingerie?

I pulled out a pink shirt and blue denim. They both were new. I got dressed up quickly. When I was applying sunscreen, Mom knocked on the door for breakfast.

'Five more minutes, Mom.' I said.

'Come out.' She said, knocking again.

I quickly applied some kohl in my eyes and wore red lipstick. I wanted to look perfect and confident.

I opened the door. The stare I got from Mom and Kaira made me realize that I was looking very different. Mom went to the kitchen to fetch breakfast for me. I sat on a chair beside Kaira. She was applying butter on a piece of bread staring at me.

'What happened?' She asked, smiling. 'Why all these?'

'I just wanted to look fresh and confident.' I said.

'Aarav is going to propose today for sure.' She giggled.

'Shut up.' I also smiled. 'He is coming here. He will teach me driving.' I informed her.

'Oh, wow!' she gave a surprised look.

'And FYI he doesn't prefer dating his boss.'

'Rubbish.' She giggled louder.

Mom came back.

'Mom, I need the car key.' I said. 'Aarav is driving me to the office today.'

'Where's he?' she asked, slowly taking the chair.

'He is coming. On the way.' I said, tearing bread with my teeth.

'He is your secretary in the office, Ella. Not your driver.'

'Mom, it's not like that.' I said. 'He won't mind.'

'Fine.' She left the table, giving a serious expression. She wasn't convinced at all.

'Is she angry?' I asked Kaira.

'Don't bother.' She replied.

Mom came back with the key. 'Keep the key to yourself. Your Dad may not need it anymore. And learn driving please.'

I nodded.

My phone rang up after sometimes. Aarav called from downstairs. Mom asked me to call him up. Initially, he refused to come up, but he had no other option.

He touched Mom's feet, followed by *Dadi*'s. He greeted Kaira with a polite smile. And glanced at me with big round eyes. Kaira was having fun. She was smiling, looking at him and me.

Mom made a special tea for him. He was hesitant at first but finished it with gentle sips. I admired his behavior with my family. Was it because we had something in between? Or it was just his respect towards his boss' family?

We left home at 9 am. He got into the driver's seat without opening the door for me. That's good. Why would he? I opened the door myself and got in.

'You really wanna learn driving from me?' he asked, starting the car.

'Yes.' I said, wearing a seatbelt. He also put the seatbelt on. We left our housing complex soon.

I was silently sitting beside him while he explained the features of the car to me. He started with the ignition to the acceleration, brake....steering control... I started losing my consciousness and only stared at him.

'Are you even listening?'

'Huh?'

'Are you even listening?' he asked again.

Well, the first time also I heard him but I couldn't react.

'Ye..ah.'

'Nah,' He said, 'you weren't. You were staring at my face.'

His eyes were on the road all the time. I looked outside.

'Why were you staring at my face?' he said.

'I didn't.'

He giggled. I forced myself not to look at him anymore.

'We are almost there.' he said. His tone completely changed.

'Fine.' I said without looking at him.

He giggled again. Now for what?

And why was I humiliating myself?

Nothing much had changed in office. Everyone congratulated me - even the watchman and the cleaner. I moved to my cabin. For three more days, nothing much happened. The doctors didn't allow me to meet Dad. Aarav drove me to the office every day. I didn't learn driving much, but I came to know a lot about him.

For a moment, I had thought that everything was solved. MUSE would not face any more problems. The smuggler would not think about smuggling again, seeing Dad's condition. At least he was a human, and he certainly would have a heart. But I would catch him anyhow and punish him for my Dad's condition.

Kailash's notice period was served, so he left the job. We gave him a proper farewell. Okay, I gave him a proper farewell. But nothing seemed well in the office. Kailash's vacant seat was troubling me a lot. My gut feeling was saying that he was innocent.

On the fourth day, we visited the hospital together. I mean to say Aarav and I. Dad was transferred to a normal cabin.

'Don't let him stress much. Just normal talk.' The nurse told me. I nodded.

Dad was kept in a separate cabin. He was alone when we entered. His eyes were closed.

'Dad.' I called him softly. He opened his eyes. And smiled. That melted my heart.

'They were not letting you come?' Dad smiled, putting his hand on my hair. He almost ruffled my hair.

'They are bad people.' I complained.

'They are just doing their jobs.'

He looked at Aarav now. Well, Dad realized his existence when he asked how he was doing.

'I'm fine.' Dad said to him. 'So, your new boss is not pressurizing you, right? You can always complain to me.'

Dad and Aarav laughed together.

'What's this? Why are you teaming up with him, Dad?'

Dad pulled me closer to hug.

The nurse came in. She looked at me once. I also scanned her.

'Dad, who do you think behind all these?' I asked after the nurse left.

'The one who returns to MUSE after office hour.' He said, smiling.

'What?' I looked at Dad. Then at Aarav. He was equally puzzled. He was staring blankly at Dad's face.

'It's not possible to smuggle in broad daylight.' Dad said. 'It happens at night. That's what my mind is saying.'

'You mean to say that somebody has a duplicate key?' I asked Dad.

'There are two keys. One with Aarav and the other one is with the watchman. If it's not Aarav, then the watchman's key is used for such jobs.' Dad said.

'The watchman didn't even say anything ever.' I said.

'He's dishonest.' Aarav spoke up. 'Remember, you asked him to give you a report of everyone's in and out time? He never showed up with one single report.'

'Right.' I said. 'I thought he is just lazy. He looks so innocent.'

'I am not sleeping in the hospital idle.' Dad said. 'My brain is working. I thought a lot, and I conclude that someone among those three, Ali, Nehal, and Kailash come back office at night. They smuggle things from Ali's account, keep the report in Nehal's computer, which is always password protected because Nehal likes to keep it protected. This way, the culprit is playing with us. He is making a mess in our brain.'

'Kailash?' I mumbled.

'Anyone can do it.' Dad said.

'So, what should we do now?' I said. 'We can't charge anyone without proof. Plus, Kailash is already off.'

'Right.' Dad and Aarav said together.

'MUSE is accessed at night. Remember what the food stall owner had said? That MUSE is opened at night often.' I whispered to Aarav. He nodded.

The nurse came in again.

'Visiting time is over.' She said loudly.

'Go to the office.' Dad said to us.

We nodded.

Aarav had brought fruits for Dad. He gave it to the nurse who inspected the fruits carefully before putting it in a basket.

'Get well soon, sir. MUSE's founder's day is near. We need you there.' Aarav said.

MUSE's founder day was on 15th April. I checked the calendar at Dad's bedside table. Two weeks left.

'I'll be at parking.' Aarav said to me and left the cabin. I nodded.

'Ma'am, please go. Leave the patient alone.' The nurse said. She refused to move away.

I kissed Dad's forehead and got up to leave. I was at the door when he called me.

'Yes, Dad?' I turned back.

'He looks more handsome than the portrait.' Dad's face was lightning with mischief.

'Huh...? Wha... What portrait?'

'Aarav's portrait.' He said. I was speechless. I stared at him- expressionless.

'Kaira is never good at hiding. Why did you trust her even?' he laughed now.

'Dad, it's nothing...' I was ashamed to face him even. 'It's nothing, okay. Take some rest.' I opened the door to leave.

'He is a nice guy, Ella. Don't lose him.' He shouted and got scolded by the nurse the next second.

I ran towards the lift. I pressed the button hard. My heart was beating fast and I was sweating. Dad knew everything already. Dad liked him! I found my hands shivering. I smiled. I couldn't suppress the joy. Nobody could separate Aarav from me now. Nothing could separate us. I didn't notice when my smile turned into loud laughter. I was laughing wholeheartedly in an empty lift that was going down in speed.

It suddenly opened, reaching the ground floor. Well, it had reached its destination. People who were waiting for the lift were staring at my face. At first, I didn't understand why I was getting such stares. Then I realized that I was laughing loudly in an EMPTY lift!

I quickly made my way out. I reached the parking. Aarav was standing leaning against the car. The joy was still on my face.

'What happened? The nurse gave you a friendship band or what?'

I laughed out loud. 'You are funny. Let's get in.'

'That's right. But what happened to you?' he asked, getting in.

'I am happy.'

'Why? Your Dad fixed your marriage?'

'Shut up.' I said. I stopped laughing. I fixed my hair with my hands and sat quietly with a smile on my face.

'Wear seatbelt.' He ordered. I put on the seatbelt. While doing that I glanced at him once.

'Aarav.' I called softly.

'Say, Ma'am.' He said, putting the reverse gear.

'Can I drive?'

He stopped the car.

'You are scaring me now. What actually happened?'

'You don't want to know that.'

'Fine.' He said, and put the car off.

'What happened now?' I asked him puzzled.

'Until and unless you are telling me what happened, I am not putting it on.' He took the keys out and put it in his pocket. Somebody honked behind.

'Are you crazy? People are honking behind. This is a hospital.'

'If you care so much tell me what happened?'

'It's not about you.'

'It's about me only. That's why I am asking.' Somebody honked again.

'Aarav, there may be a serious patient in that car. Drive, please.' I folded my hands. He sat idle. 'Okay, it's about you. I'll tell you everything.'

'Sure?'

'Yes.'

He took the key out and put the car on again. We left the hospital.

'Tell me.'

'Okay,' I breathed out. 'Dad knows about us.'

The car stopped in the middle of nowhere. And then bump! Another car hit it from behind. Thanks to the seatbelts that saved us from sure death. I took a few seconds to think about what had happened.

'Are you serious?' his face was worried.

'Are you seriously getting into an accident?' I shouted at him. 'This car didn't even cross a year. And we could be dead by now.'

'Hey, *behenchod*, move on...' the driver from that car shouted on us. 'You better pay me for my loss. Are you dreaming?' his door opened. He was probably coming out. Few bikes also started to assemble on the road.

'What the fuck! Aarav!' I shouted again. 'Drive!' He put the engine on again. We drove. We drove for half an hour. We didn't know where we are. Finally, he stopped at an open ground. It was lakeside. He got out of the car. I followed.

He was inspecting the damage. I also went back. We sighed together. We looked at each other. We stared in our eyes for a few moments and burst out to laugh.

'What the fuck did you do to my father's car?' I laughed some more.

'How the fuck your father came to know about us?' he continued laughing. 'You seriously had almost sent me to a cardiac arrest.'

'Sorry.' I went quiet for a second and laughed again.

'How will I face him now?'

'It's fine. He likes you.' I said.

'Really?' he went quiet completely.

'Yes. Kaira had given me a portrait of you. Dad somehow discovered that and guessed the rest.' I said.

He kept quiet.

'C'mon Aarav we don't need to bother about anything now. Dad likes you.'

'But I don't do my boss. No... never.' He said. 'Get in the car, please. I will take it to the garage. You can take a cab from there.'

I went numb.

I got in, and he drove to the garage. We remained silent all the while.

'Make the bills in the company's account.' I said before getting in the cab.

Aarav was overacting. And why not? I had hurt him earlier. Unintentionally though.

xxii

My mood was off. I reached the office and saw the watchman sleeping on his chair. I felt like pouring water on his head. If Dad's doubt was right, I would fire him before anything else.

I walked inside. Everyone looked at me once. Some of them greeted as well I guessed. I didn't look at them. I dropped my handbag on the table and went to the bathroom to freshen up. Aarav had erased the joy from my face completely. He came to the office in the second half and slammed the bill on my table.

I was going through the bill when I received a call. I was a little surprised because he didn't call me in the office hour ever.

'Hey, Shadab. How are you?' I said on the phone.

'I'm fine, sister. What about you? By the way, congratulations on being the new CEO of MUSE.' He said.

'I'm fine. And thanks.' I said. 'Dad has put a great responsibility on me, Shadab.'

'Indeed, a great one.' He said. 'But I am really very happy about the decision uncle has taken.'

'Do you think I deserved this?'

'Yes, indeed. I was in the sea when I used to go there. It's huge.' He laughed. 'Not my thing. I'll join some job.'

'You can come to MUSE even.' I said.

'No, Mom was saying that I should become serious about a job now.' He said.

I understood the point. I knew his Mom would never send him here again. She had always dreamt of seeing him as the next CEO of MUSE.

'Okay. Do whatever you like to do.' I said.

'Yeah. How's Uncle?'

'Better.'

'Okay, I'm hanging up. You better focus on office. And don't be nervous.'

I smiled. But I was not happy.

The day passed like that. The car was in the garage. I had to take an auto home. I could have taken a cab as well but I didn't feel like waiting for the cab. Aarav went home after me because he was working on some accounts file.

The next day was dull in the office. I was sad because I couldn't solve the mystery. I was sad because Aarav was offended with me. I was sad because I needed Dad so much in this situation. I was sad because Mom had scolded me repeated times for the car. I had lied to her that I was driving. She shouted at me for driving without a license. And I was sad because I had to attend a meeting with the suppliers. Shukla was one of them.

At noon, the meeting was held in our board room. I was tired of their questions. Nobody was ready to believe in our business strategies. Nobody could trust us anymore. Actually, nobody could trust me. They needed Dad. However, nobody broke a deal. That was the only positive thing that happened for MUSE. They gave us another chance. We couldn't pay our suppliers for the next few months as our resources were limited. I had a big fear of losing deals, but it didn't happen.

What happened was depressing for me. I poured a cup of coffee for myself as I didn't get tea at that hour and headed towards my cabin when I heard something. Well, overheard something.

'I don't know how Mr. Malik could handover the company to his baby girl? Do you think she understands anything of business, let alone hardware?' a laughing Shukla said to Shinde, another supplier.

Shinde smiled sarcastically, 'Women don't understand business. They are better in the kitchen.'

'Mr. Malik is really getting old, and his brain needs some rest. This is just a blatant decision. In two years...' Shukla wiggled two fingers at Shinde and whispered, 'I guarantee you, she will close the company and get back to her kitchen space. I have seen many like this.'

The cup in my hand was shivering. The coffee in it was experiencing a terrible earthquake. My brain matters were fuming. I took a deep breath and appeared in front of them.

'Mr. Shinde and Mr. Shukla, with due respect, you should not talk rubbish about me standing at my office premises. At least, have the minimum sense of going out and talk about my actual place – the company or the kitchen.'

Within a moment, they evacuated the place. I didn't like the taste of the coffee anymore. I threw it in the sink and sat on my chair in my cabin.

Standing in the 21st century, we still face these kinds of rotten brains. I had every reason to get depressed. Hadn't I joined MUSE I would not have experienced the real faces of the society. The real faces in the office. The real faces in my own family!

The weekend came.

It was Sunday. Mom and Kaira were in the hospital. I was sitting on the couch in my drawing room with a cup of tea. I was stirring a sugar cube in it lazily thinking about my ill fate.

I was wearing denim shorts and a sleeveless vest. It was too hot that day. I thought of taking a bath after having tea. Then I thought Mom asks not to go to the bath after tea. I could not afford another scolding.
The doorbell suddenly rang. Mom, *Dadi*, and Kaira couldn't be back so soon. I went to open the door.

It was Haris. He was standing smiling. He had a box of sweet in his hand.

'I have good news.' He said.

'Increment?' I said, looking at the box of sweets.

'No. Try again.' He said coming in.

'Promotion?'

'Sort of. Try again. This is the last chance.' He sat on the sofa.

I gave a tough thought.

'Foreign transfer?'

'Yes.' He jumped up from the sofa and pulled me up in his arms. 'I got transferred to Canada.'

'Haris, that's great!' I laughed. In the process, the tea spilt on the floor. He put me down. I hugged him tightly. He opened the box and put a *laddoo* in my mouth.

I put one in his.

'I'll miss you.' I said.

'Get satisfied with Aarav.' He said. 'You know what, Manisha wished me luck.' We laughed. But I became quiet soon. I told him everything that happened with Aarav the other day.

'This guy is tough.' He laughed after listening to me.

I nodded. I wept on putting my head on my best friend's shoulder. That was how it ended up being a bad day, again.

It was just three days before the founder's day. Dad was released the day before. *Dadi* went back to her native home. The car was back from the garage. Aarav let me handle the steering for the first time. We weren't talking much, but he was doing his duty well.

I didn't break the car again, thankfully. I was learning.

I thought it would be another normal day. I was wrong.

I entered the office first. Amod, the cleaner was there alone. The watchman was outside the gate, though. Aarav had gone to park the car.

'Who did this? How can a person be so irresponsible? What is this?...' I found Amod shouting and abusing.

I went closer to him. He was blabbering angrily while cleaning the floor. He didn't even notice my presence.

'Amod, what happened?' I asked him.

'Madam, see.' He pointed to the floor. I looked down closely. There were ashes.

'Ash?'

'Cigarette residual, Ma'am. Somebody smoked here!' he was furious.

'You didn't clean after office yesterday?' I asked. 'I did.' He said. 'It wasn't there.'

I took a closer look at the floor. I followed the ash. Amod also came with me. Almost five to six cigarettes were burned one after another and whoever took it walked from the lobby to Ali's desk. We also found ashes near Nehal's keyboard.

'He's the smuggler.' I shouted. Aarav was just in. He stood there.

Amod went down the floor in all fours and picked something out. It was a burned-out cigarette.

'Ma'am.' He gave it to me. 'This is a no-smoking zone. How can someone smoke here?'

Aarav walked towards me. He took a look at the situation.

'What brand is it?' Aarav asked.

'Gold Flake.' I said. 'Who smokes Gold Flake here?'

'I don't know.' Aarav said. 'I didn't know that anyone of us smokes. Except you.' He whispered in my ear.

'This one is not me.' I whispered back at him with angry eyes.

He nodded.

'Amod, clean it up before anyone comes. And don't tell anything to anyone, okay?'

'Okay.' He said hesitantly.

Even the smartest criminal can make a mistake. Whoever he was, should not have smoked there. A war had started in my brain. I went in deep thought. Who could it be?

In the evening I went out of the cabin. I found Nehal in the coffee machine. He was pouring himself milk.

'Hey.' I smiled at him.

Seeing me, he composed himself. 'Good evening, Ma'am.' He greeted with an odd smile. He knew I still doubt him.

'Good evening.' I said. 'Only milk?' I pointed to the cup.

'I like milk. Nothing else.'

'Not even tea?' I asked, sipping my cup of tea that Aarav had got me a few minutes ago in my cabin.

'No.'

'Cigarette?'

'No.' He said, smiling awkwardly.

'That's great.' I said.

He left the spot after finishing his milk. I went to their cubicles. Kailash's one was empty. We were doing an interview event after the founder day to hire new employees. We might get a better one in Kailash's place. My heart still didn't believe him to be guilty until now.

'Good evening, Ma'am.' Amar greeted from his desk.

'Hey, Amar.' I said. 'Did you get the invitation email for founder's day?' I asked.

'Yes, Ma'am.' He said. 'Thanks.'

'You can bring anyone you want. It'll be a great party.'

'Sure.' He said, smiling.

'Amar, do you smoke?' I asked.

'No.' He said instantly.

'Oh. I found a cigarette in the lobby. Maybe Aarav.' I laughed, keeping an eye at him to check his expression.

'Aarav doesn't smoke, I guess. I never saw him going out to the terrace.'

'Then who goes there every day?' I played a hunch. 'I saw someone there yesterday.'

'You saw Ali.' He said. 'He is the only smoker in the office, Ma'am.'

My hands clasped against the teacup tightly. My heartbeat became faster.

Ali!

'Oh.' I smiled. 'Maybe.'

I checked his screen and found a mistake in his Java code. I corrected it and left. He thanked me, smiling.

'Aarav, Ali is the only smoker in office.' I said as soon as I entered my cabin.

'How come I don't know about this?' he mumbled.

We charged the watchman after everyone left. He swore on his mother that he didn't give the key to anyone.

I was walking alone on the road. Aarav had to leave soon, so I had asked him to take the car. I decided to take an auto. When I reached the auto stand, I found Ali. What was he doing till now? I checked my watch. He had left an hour ago.

'Hi, Ali!' I enthusiastically said to him. He was surprised to see me as if he had seen a ghost. 'Didn't go home till now?' I asked.

'No. I had to buy some medicines for my mother.' He said.

I didn't see a medical store nearby. Nor did I see any medicine in his hand. He must have been lying. Though he could put the medicine in his pocket but his face said that he was lying.

A lie is hard to keep in.

'I already bought it from the nearby lane.' He said quickly. 'Will take an auto soon. Where's your car?'

'Aarav took it home today. His Mom is not well.' I said, smiling.

'Let's walk to the auto.' He said.

'Yeah, sure.' I said.

The autos at the first of the queue were all full. We had to walk until we get an empty one.

'Ali, do you have a lighter?' I said, taking out a cigarette from my purse.

He looked at me surprised for a few seconds as if he had not seen a woman smoke. Then he shoved his hands in the pocket and took out a lighter.

'Thanks.' I said, taking it from him.

I tried to light the cigarette, but it didn't catch fire.

'May I?' He asked. We had stopped walking. He tried to lit the cigarette while I hold it between my fingers. It didn't catch fire. He touched the tip of the cigarette and smiled. 'Ma'am, the filter is wet.'

'Oh. Maybe the water bottle leaked.' I said. 'I'll buy one.' I looked at a small *pan* shop.

'It's okay. You can try mine. Though its a different brand.'

'Oh, that's fine.' I said, happily. 'Thanks.'

He took out a cigarette box and pulled out one from it. This was what I wanted to see - the brand, Gold Flake. I lit the cigarette.

'Ma'am, don't keep cigarettes with water bottles.' He smiled, putting the lighter back in his pocket.

Little did he know that I wetted the cigarette while taking it out from the bag just to check his brand. I took an auto. He took his auto. We headed to different directions. I blew the smoke outside the auto.

On the next day, I woke up early and gave medicines to Dad. He was still very weak. I fed him to breakfast with my hands. I found tears in his eyes. He was emotional always.

'You know, Ella, when you were born, my colleagues and friends mocked me for having a daughter. Even when Kaira was born and we decided that we won't take another kid, everyone forced me to have a son.' He said, 'but your Mom and I decided that you two are everything to us. We don't need a son.'

I stared at Dad. He smiled and continued. 'Now my friends say that I have got sons in my daughters. I don't understand what they mean. Why do you need a son? Why do you have to call your daughter 'a son' when they do something great?'

I smiled, hugging him. 'You are my strength, Dad. I always wanted to be you. I promise I'll fix everything with MUSE.'

'You will. You can.' He said. 'Even if I die today I'll die happy because you are there to take care of everything.'

'Shut up, Dad.' I hugged him.

He patted my back smiling.

'I love you so much, Dad.' I said, wiping tears of emotions, 'please get well soon.'

I fed him the rest of the food. We talked about a lot of things - Haris' transfer, Kaira's future, MUSE's new recruitment plan, and the founder's day party.

Aarav had called to inform me that he was getting out of the home to pick me up.

I thought for a second and replied, 'Don't come. I need to go somewhere before going to the office.'

'Where? I mean, if you can say.' He demanded.

'To Kailash's house.' I said.

'What? Why?'
'It's part of the investigation. You want to go?'
'Sure. I think I am Watson. I should go.'
'I'll pick you up.'

xxiii

Founder's Day

Mom drove Kaira and Dad to the party. It was held in a banquet hall every year. The last two days were hectic for me. I have never worked that much in my entire life. I had to prepare for my speech. Every year I listened to Dad sitting in the front seat beside Mom and Kaira. This year I would be in Dad's place and Dad in mine. I finally got out of home at 8 pm with Haris. He was scheduled to pick me up from home.

I was dressed in a thigh-length black full sleeve dress. I wore Mom's diamond necklace and matching earrings. I put on my new black heels.

'You look ravishingly awesome.' Haris commented when I got into the car.

'Thanks.' I said.

'So, are you ready with the speech?'

'Yes.' I said.

'All the best.' He said.

I put my left leg on the right. I had done full body waxing for the first time, and it felt great. It was like all the cells in my body were active. I combed my hair once before getting out of the car. Haris helped me with that.

I entered the venue with an uncomfortable pair of heels and a racing heartbeat. There were almost two hundred people. Important customers, suppliers, staff, ex-staff, their families, and my family, of course. Some people liked me, some hated.

Aarav received me like a perfect secretary. His Mom was also present. I smiled at her, folding my hands and uttering, *'Namaste'* to her. She nodded, smiling. Amar greeted me. He was there with his parents and sister. Ali was sitting with his parents as well. Kailash was also there with his mother. We had sent him an invitation as well.

'You are late.' Mom whispered to me when I reached there.

'Just five minutes late, Mom.' I said.

'Okay, you can leave your bag to me.' She said, holding my bag.

'No. I need it.' I said.

Dad accompanied me to the stage. I held his hand. Dad announced my takeover again in front of everyone. He gave a small speech on the success of the company so far. He also mentioned about the mishaps and promised that it wouldn't change anything. It wouldn't affect the suppliers and customers. They could still trust us. They could place trust in me.

He handed the microphone to me. Kaira helped him step off the stage. She was also looking gorgeous. Her fair complexion was shining in the light. She was wearing a red maxi dress. She didn't wear her spectacle. Instead, she used blue lenses that looked perfect on her.

'Hi, Good evening, ladies and gentlemen!' I started with the mike. 'Many of you do not know me until now. I am Farya Malik, the CEO of the Modernus Enterprise. I thank my father for trusting me this far. I promise to solve the issues with the company within a short period. In fact…,' I stopped. I scanned the crowd. It was time. Yes, I needed to be confident enough to expose everything I got to know in the past two days. I looked at Aarav. He was standing at a corner in the hall. He showed me a thumbs-up sign which meant 'go-ahead'. So, I continued, '…in fact, I should solve it now.'

Every pair of eyes turned to me. I went nervous for a moment. Aarav gestured me to continue. I looked at my parents. They were puzzled. Even Kaira was staring at me intensely.

'When I joined MUSE, I didn't expect to see the bad side of it in the first month only.' I started to speak slowly. 'I had thought that things would get better. But it didn't. It took the worst turn.' I stopped. My parents' eyes were fixed on me. 'Things went missing. Somebody abused me in broad daylight. Laptops went missing. Customers came with demands for money for the lost items. And finally, my Dad got a heart attack.' My voice became heavy. I controlled myself. 'The last one was the most unexpected, and it hurt my family and me. It gave immense pain to every one of us.' I said, 'Okay, I didn't prepare all of these in my speech. I had prepared a sober one, a formal one. But when I got up on this stage today, I realized that I should expose the person who is responsible for all of these. That one single person who made my life hell in the past few months and smuggled for a year. The person who is responsible for MUSE's financial downfall.'

There was pin-drop silence in the hall. Kailash's face was pale. Amar's was confused, and Nehal looked blankly at me. Ali sat straight.

'Who is it?' Dad said. He was sweating. Kaira held his hand tightly.

'Dad trusted you the most, right?' I said, looking straight. Every pair of eyes looked at the place where the staff was sitting. 'Ali?'

There was a gasping sound in the hall. Everyone was shocked.

'What?' Dad and Ali said together. Except for Aarav, everyone was quite surprised as if they didn't believe their ears.

'Yes, Dad. Ali is the one who is behind all of these.' I said.

'Do you have proof, Ma'am?' Ali shouted in rage. He stood from his seat. His parents were also up.

'Yes, I do have.' I said firmly.

'What do you have?' he asked. His voice had raised so much that it hurt my ears.

'Ali was smuggling things under Dad's nose for a long time. There was a transaction file maintained by Ali personally. The transaction was done under my name. Only my name was used - nothing else. When I came to the office, Ali understood that it was not very easy to fool me. He tried to threaten me through Kailash. He even tampered Nehal's computer abusing me. I didn't lose hope even after such humiliation. I stayed. I never doubted him because Dad trusted him the most, and he always behaved well with me.'

'Why would Kailash do whatever I say?' Ali shouted.

'Because you blackmailed him.' I answered. 'He had taken money from you, which he couldn't pay on time. In fact, he could never pay it to you. You made him do all of these to pardon him from giving you the money. In fact, you needed a cover for your evil works. You needed a person to take the responsibilities for the lost items.'

'You are lying.' He shouted. 'Ask Kailash. He is sitting right here.' He moved towards Kailash, 'hey, tell everything...'

'Wait up, Ali.' I said. 'Let me finish.'

He stopped. He was still fuming. Kailash was so worried that he started shivering.

'You asked Kailash to take the blame on him. When he did so, he didn't take the blame for everything. He only confessed about two RAMs that went missing at that time. Not about anything else, not about abusing me and tampering Nehal's computer. You saw that things didn't work well. You started threatening him to quit MUSE. He was forced, and finally, he did so. That's where my doubt began. Aarav told me that this job was Kailash's last hope to run his family. I believed that there was someone behind him. I found a file in Nehal's computer and believed that he was the culprit. But no, you put the file in Nehal's computer one night, as you always come to MUSE at night with a duplicate key that you got a year ago by duplicating the watchman's key without his notice. The food stall owner on the other side often found MUSE opened at night. You chose Nehal's computer because it was the only one with password protection. You thought that the file will never come up. And if it does, Nehal will be blamed. You played wrong, Ali. You actually should have not kept the records in office. You tried to play with me. You tried to secure the file on his computer as it was password protected. I checked his computer because of the same reason.

When I asked Nehal about it, he denied. He was innocent and didn't know anything about such activities. Aarav even saw him once talking to random people. Well, they were his uncles who used to come to meet him in office. Because of some family issues, Nehal's family is not connected to his uncles. Aarav saw Nehal talking to a man with two laptop bags the day before we realized that two laptops were missing from Ali's account and one from Nehal's. It was another reason why I doubted him, but it was purely his personal belongings.' I stopped to breathe.

The hall was silent, including the staff.

'Three days ago, I found Amod shouting in rage while cleaning the floor. There were cigarette ashes on the floor. You did mistake again. You actually had taken it so casually now. You thought that I can never get to you. Well, we even discovered a burned Gold Flake. I came to know from Amar that you are the only one who smokes in the whole office.' I continued, 'for the first time, my doubt went on you. Later, you know what happened in the auto stand. That night, I played with you. I intentionally wetted my cigarette to check yours.

Two things got clear that night. Number one, you smoke. Number two, you smoke the brand we got on the office floor.'

'So, the cigarette is the proof?' Ali laughed madly.

'No.' I said. 'I knew what I have to do. I went to Kailash's home. I pressurized him and assured him that he would not be in trouble if he tells me the truth. I also assured him that he will get his job back with a hike if he tells the truth.'

Ali's eyes were on Kailash. They were fuming. Kailash left the chair and stood up. Dad also left the chair.

'Ali, Kailash confessed everything and told me everything about you. Whatever I said it's true.' I said. I put a hand in my bag and pulled out my phone. I connected it to the laptop and played the video where I had recorded Kailash's statement. The video played in a large projector connected to the laptop. Every pair of eyes were on it.

Everyone was still as if they were fixed by some alien force. The video went on. Everyone was watching and listening to it carefully. Before it ended, Ali jumped on Kailash and grabbed him by his collar. It shocked everyone. There was huge chaos. Dad was shivering. He sat on the chair, holding his head. Kaira and Mom got busy with him.

'Ali, there's no use of it.' I said. 'Stop.'

He didn't stop. We had already informed the cop. Mr. Bose had made contact, and I already had handed the video to the police. Mr. Bose came in with a police officer who grabbed Ali by his wrist and separated him from Kailash.

I didn't hear anything after that. There was chaos. There were muffled voices. I went to Dad. I hugged him tightly to console him.

'I still can't believe this. Ali?' Dad wept, 'Why did he do this?'

'Greed, Dad. You only say. It's a king's business.'

Ali was taken by the cops. His parents left as well. Kailash's mother almost touched my feet for saving his son and giving back his job. Haris was still shocked. He didn't expect to witness such a long drama where I played the protagonist.

Aarav smiled at me.

Okay, wait… this is not exactly the end.

The party was not the same anymore. I knew Dad would take time to recover from the shock. Mom and Kaira were taking good care of him. Even they witnessed a perfect drama in front of their eyes. I took care of the party. People started to eat and drink slowly. Basically, they were gossiping in low decibel. Whatever happened in my company so far was enough for them to discuss over coffee and tea for almost a month. People got content for gossiping. Anyway, that's social work from our side. So, I took it positively.

I grabbed a glass of wine and took a small sip from it. My eyes searched for Aarav. I found his mother sitting with Mom, Dad, and Kaira. I went to the parking.

'Searching for someone?' a voice came from behind. I quickly turned back.

'What are you doing here? I was searching for you only.' I said, smiling boldly.

'Just inhaling some fresh air.' He said.

'I also need it badly.' I said.

'I didn't know that you can carry this out so well. I thought you would just deliver your prepared speech and fire Ali after the party.'

'I did it little publicly, I know.' I laughed.

'Moron.' I abused Ali. 'He broke Dad's trust.'

'People can go to any extent for money, Ella.' He said.

'Right, Aarav.' I spoke up, leaning against a random car that was parked. 'He could have earned more if he worked harder and used his brain in the right place. Such a greedy asshole.'

'People generally go for the easier way.' He said.

I nodded.

'I have heard that the terrace of this banquet is very nice.' He said.

'Let's go.' I started walking.

'Where?' He asked. 'Terrace?'

'Yes.' I said, removing my heels. We didn't take the lift. We started climbing the staircase. I was ahead of him.

'Can I ask you something?' he asked from behind.

'Go ahead.' I said.

'Why didn't you ever doubt me? I could also be the person behind all these.'

I stopped as we reached the terrace. I turned to him. I was holding my heels in one hand and the bag on the other. In the process, I lost the wine glass. I forgot where I kept it.

'Because I had a soft feeling for you from the very beginning. Technically I thought that it could be you but never convinced my mind to think further.'

He smiled, looking down.

I looked around. The terrace was nice. The view of the city from the terrace was amazing. I went to the extreme end of the terrace. He followed me and stood beside me.

I dropped my heels and bag on the terrace floor.

'So what is your next plan? What are you going to do?' he asked.

'I... I don't know... well, I know...' I started blabbering as usual. 'You know what I want to do the next?' I moved towards him. 'I want to do this.' The distance between us was zero by now. I pulled him by his collar and grabbed his lips with mine. It happened so fast that he forgot to close his eyes even. I increased the intensity of the kiss. He started to cooperate. He grabbed me by my waist and pulled me to his body. We shared the warmth of each other's breath and body.

We sat on the terrace floor kissing. Actually, smooching.

We released each other slowly after a minute that felt like forever. I opened my eyes to look at his. He was smiling. He looked content. He stared at my eyes deeply.

'What?' I whispered.

'I think you said that you don't do your staff?' he said in a hoarse voice.

'Yes, right, you are.' I put my hand inside my bag, which was there beside me all the time. I pulled out a paper.

'I don't do my staff. In fact, I hate relationships in business.'

He looked puzzled. I hold the paper in front of his face. He took it.

'What's it?' he questioned, trying to figure it out in the dark.

'Your release letter. You are released from MUSE with good conduct, and it ends today evening. You are no more my staff, Aarav Shenoy.'

He was surprised. He paused.

'Go, do your MBA. Fulfil your dream. The company will provide you with a scholarship. Though you don't need it, I know. You are very rich by now.' I giggled.

'Yes I am.' he said. 'Because I fell in love for the first time. And I didn't make a mistake. I'm quite rich in love.'

We laughed together.

'I have a serious question.' He said.

'Shoot.' I said.

'You have literally fired me from my job. What will happen to my Mom? How will we buy tea bags when you visit home?'

'That's my responsibility until your MBA ends.' I said.

'This is getting insane.' He giggled. 'Are these even real?'

'Now, I have a serious question.' I said.

'Go ahead.' He said, pulling me closer.

'I am elder to you. You don't have a problem, right? Plus, I am enhanced in a career than you. There will be no status problem, right? I mean, you won't think that you are inferior to me, right?'

He chuckled. 'I love you for whatever you are. If you are the most deserving boss, I am the most deserving lover in the world.

We giggled together.

'I love you, Aarav.'

'I love you too, Ella.'

I lowered my eyes. He grabbed me close for a hug. Soon the hug turned out to another intimate kiss.

Somewhere, far far away, a cracker burst in the sky lighting it up.

* 9 7 8 8 1 9 4 3 7 0 5 2 9 *